A LUCKY LUKE ADVENTURE

THE BOUNTY HUNTER

BY MORRIS & GOSCINNY

CINEBOOK

Original title: Lucky Luke – Chasseur de primes

Original edition: © Dargaud Editeur Paris 1972 by Goscinny and Morris
© Lucky Comics
www.lucky-luke.com

Lettering and text layout: Imadjinn sarl
Printed in Spain by Just Colour Graphic

This edition published in Great Britain in 2010 by
Cinebook Ltd
56 Beech Avenue
Canterbury, Kent
CT4 7TA
www.cinebook.com

A CIP catalogue record for this book
is available from the British Library

ISBN 978-1-84918-059-7

9th CINEBOOK
The 9th Art Publisher

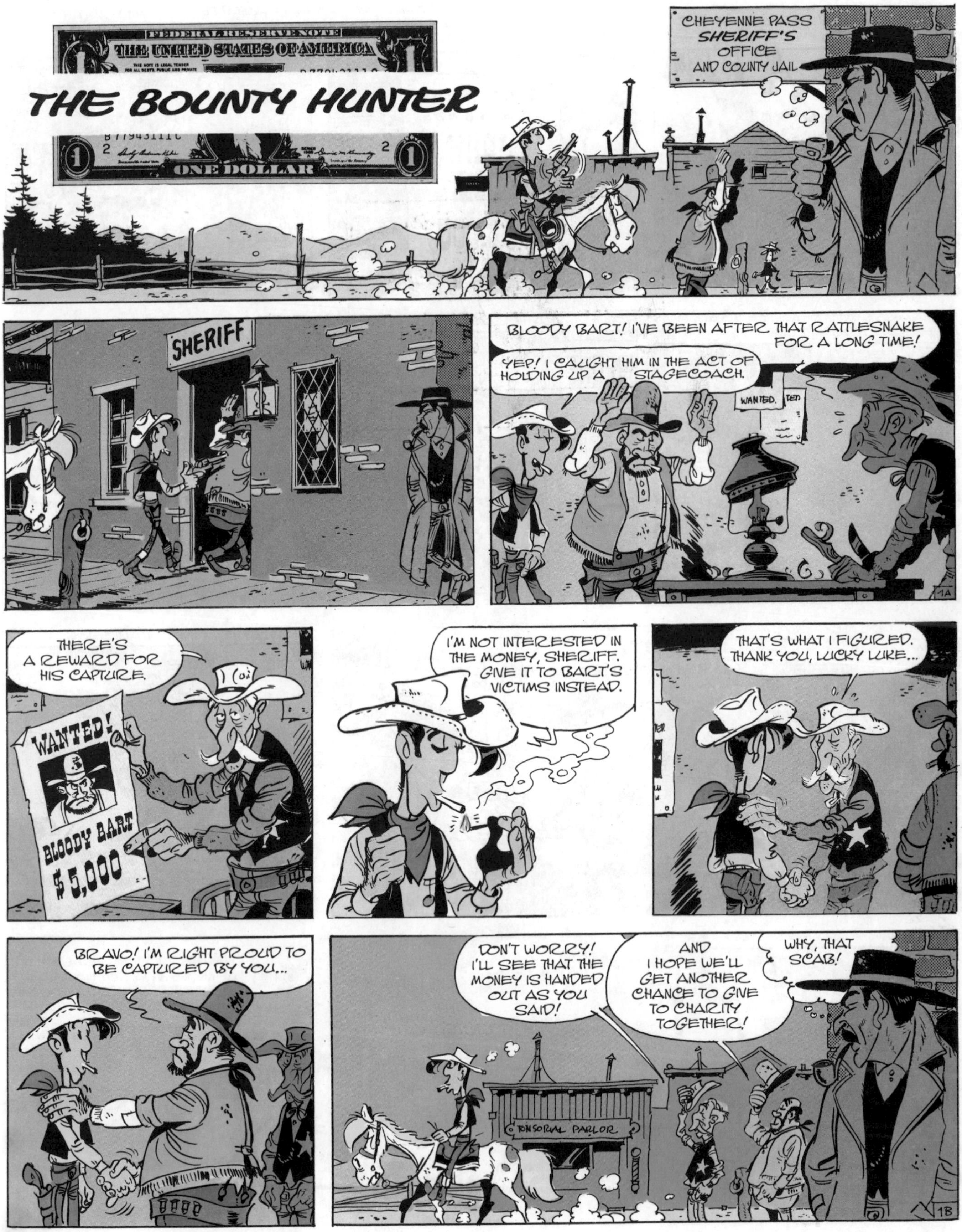
FEDERAL RESERVE NOTE
THE UNITED STATES OF AMERICA
THE BOUNTY HUNTER
ONE DOLLAR
CHEYENNE PASS SHERIFF'S OFFICE AND COUNTY JAIL
SHERIFF
BLOODY BART! I'VE BEEN AFTER THAT RATTLESNAKE FOR A LONG TIME!
YEP! I CAUGHT HIM IN THE ACT OF HOLDING UP A STAGECOACH.
WANTED.
THERE'S A REWARD FOR HIS CAPTURE.
WANTED!
BLOODY BART
$ 5,000
I'M NOT INTERESTED IN THE MONEY, SHERIFF. GIVE IT TO BART'S VICTIMS INSTEAD.
THAT'S WHAT I FIGURED. THANK YOU, LUCKY LUKE...
BRAVO! I'M RIGHT PROUD TO BE CAPTURED BY YOU...
DON'T WORRY! I'LL SEE THAT THE MONEY IS HANDED OUT AS YOU SAID!
AND I HOPE WE'LL GET ANOTHER CHANCE TO GIVE TO CHARITY TOGETHER!
WHY, THAT SCAB!
TONSORIAL PARLOR

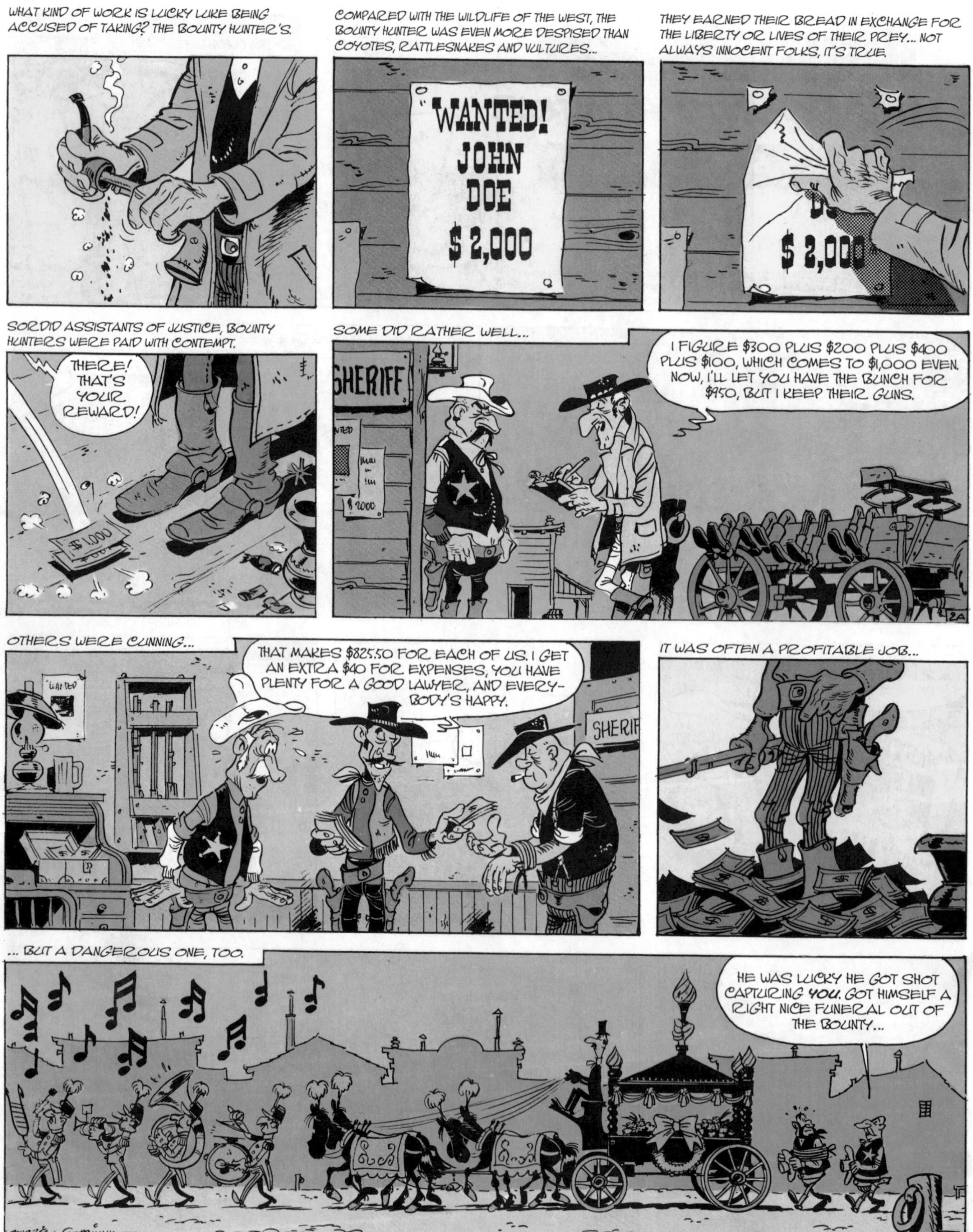
WHAT KIND OF WORK IS LUCKY LUKE BEING ACCUSED OF TAKING? THE BOUNTY HUNTER'S.
COMPARED WITH THE WILDLIFE OF THE WEST, THE BOUNTY HUNTER WAS EVEN MORE DESPISED THAN COYOTES, RATTLESNAKES AND VULTURES...
WANTED! JOHN DOE $ 2,000
THEY EARNED THEIR BREAD IN EXCHANGE FOR THE LIBERTY OR LIVES OF THEIR PREY... NOT ALWAYS INNOCENT FOLKS, IT'S TRUE.
$ 2,000
SORDID ASSISTANTS OF JUSTICE, BOUNTY HUNTERS WERE PAID WITH CONTEMPT.
THERE! THAT'S YOUR REWARD!
SOME DID RATHER WELL...
SHERIFF
I FIGURE $300 PLUS $200 PLUS $400 PLUS $100, WHICH COMES TO $1,000 EVEN. NOW, I'LL LET YOU HAVE THE BUNCH FOR $950, BUT I KEEP THEIR GUNS.
OTHERS WERE CUNNING...
THAT MAKES $825.50 FOR EACH OF US. I GET AN EXTRA $40 FOR EXPENSES, YOU HAVE PLENTY FOR A GOOD LAWYER, AND EVERYBODY'S HAPPY.
IT WAS OFTEN A PROFITABLE JOB...
... BUT A DANGEROUS ONE, TOO.
HE WAS LUCKY HE GOT SHOT CAPTURING **YOU**. GOT HIMSELF A RIGHT NICE FUNERAL OUT OF THE BOUNTY...

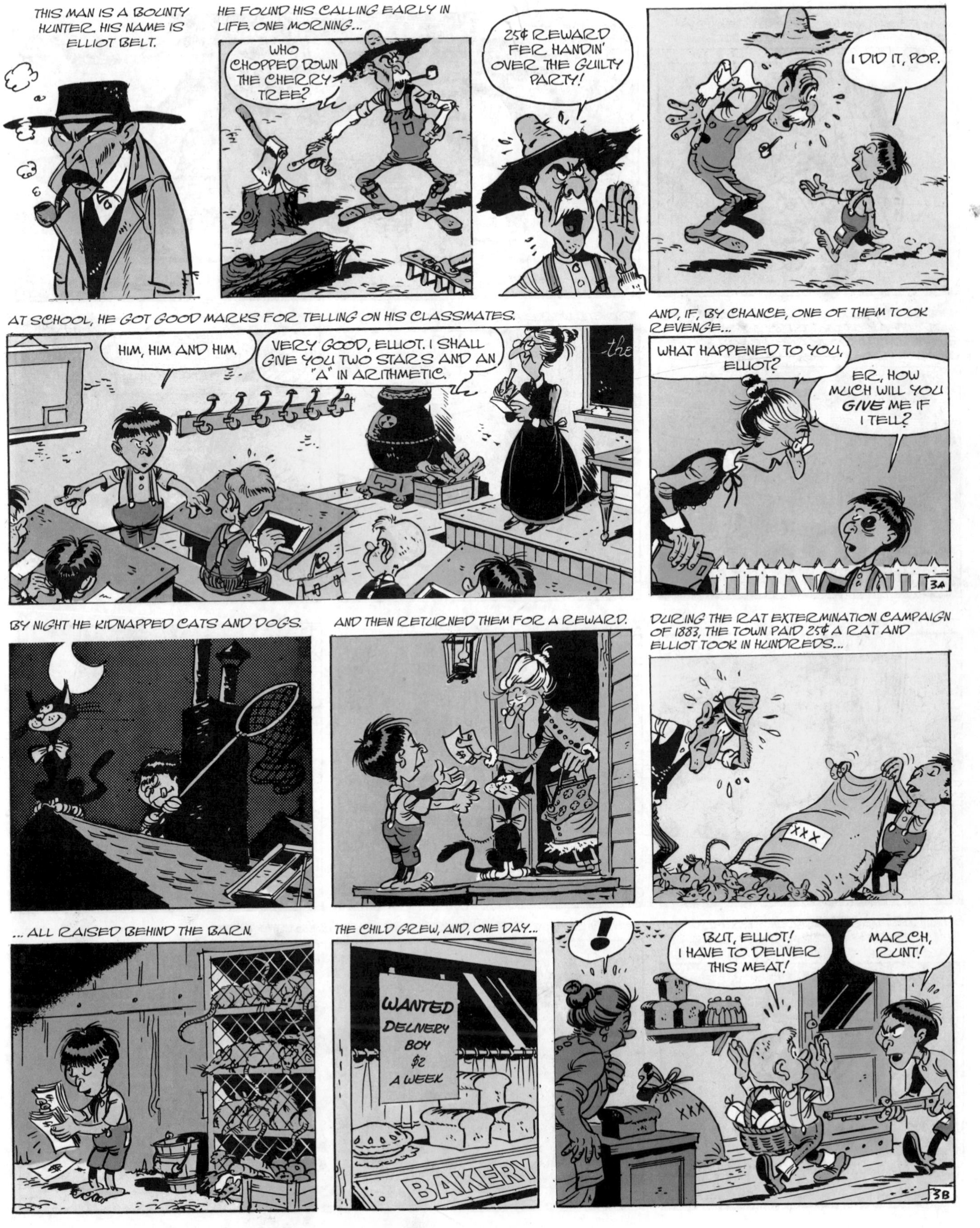
THIS MAN IS A BOUNTY HUNTER. HIS NAME IS ELLIOT BELT.
HE FOUND HIS CALLING EARLY IN LIFE. ONE MORNING...
WHO CHOPPED DOWN THE CHERRY TREE?
25¢ REWARD FER HANDIN' OVER THE GUILTY PARTY!
I DID IT, POP.
AT SCHOOL, HE GOT GOOD MARKS FOR TELLING ON HIS CLASSMATES.
HIM, HIM AND HIM.
VERY GOOD, ELLIOT. I SHALL GIVE YOU TWO STARS AND AN "A" IN ARITHMETIC.
AND, IF, BY CHANCE, ONE OF THEM TOOK REVENGE...
WHAT HAPPENED TO YOU, ELLIOT?
ER, HOW MUCH WILL YOU GIVE ME IF I TELL?
BY NIGHT HE KIDNAPPED CATS AND DOGS.
AND THEN RETURNED THEM FOR A REWARD.
DURING THE RAT EXTERMINATION CAMPAIGN OF 1883, THE TOWN PAID 25¢ A RAT AND ELLIOT TOOK IN HUNDREDS...
XXX
... ALL RAISED BEHIND THE BARN.
THE CHILD GREW, AND, ONE DAY...
WANTED DELIVERY BOY $2 A WEEK
BAKERY
!
BUT, ELLIOT! I HAVE TO DELIVER THIS MEAT!
MARCH, RUNT!
XXX

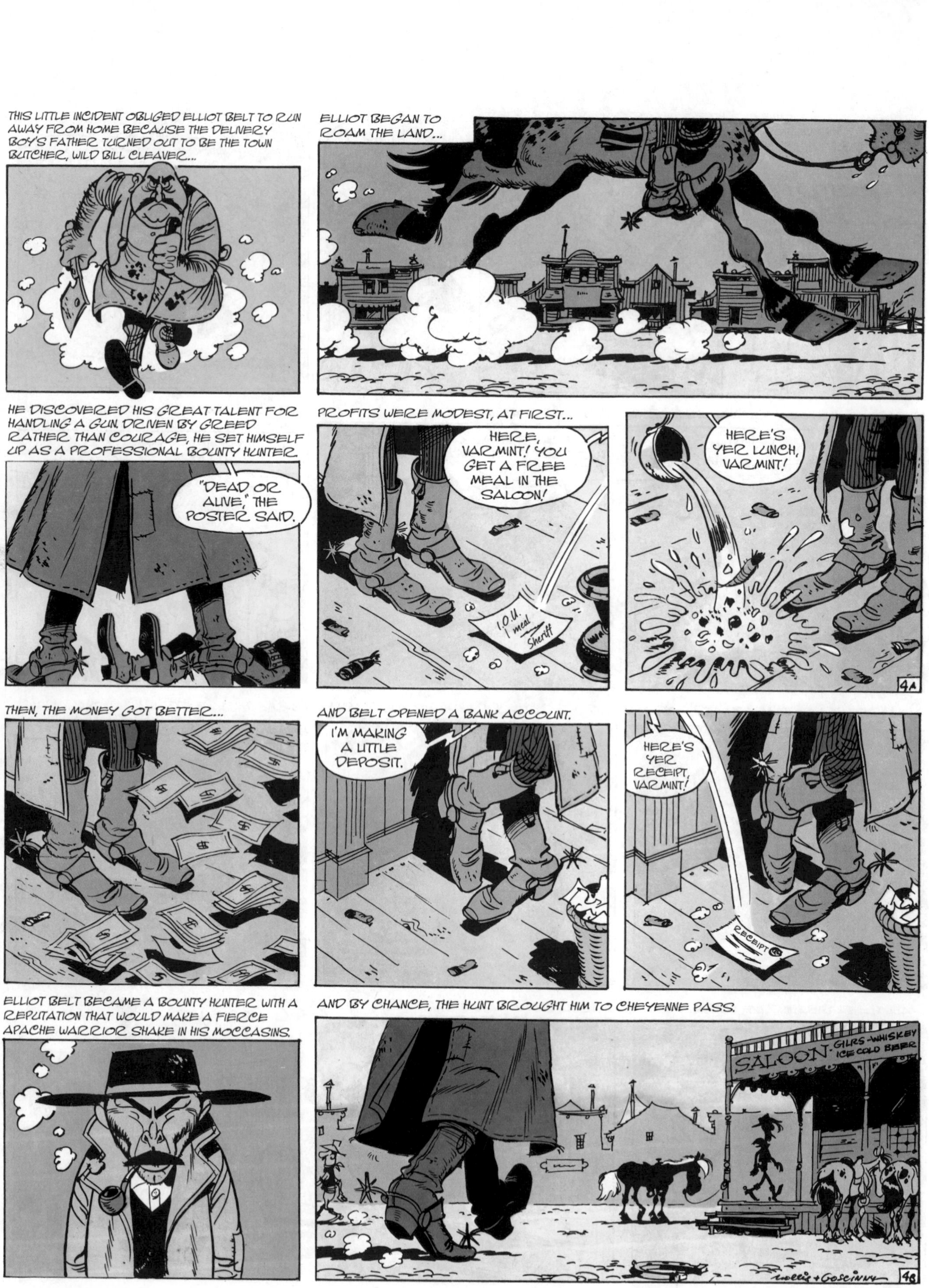
THIS LITTLE INCIDENT OBLIGED ELLIOT BELT TO RUN AWAY FROM HOME BECAUSE THE DELIVERY BOY'S FATHER TURNED OUT TO BE THE TOWN BUTCHER, WILD BILL CLEAVER...
ELLIOT BEGAN TO ROAM THE LAND...
HE DISCOVERED HIS GREAT TALENT FOR HANDLING A GUN. DRIVEN BY GREED RATHER THAN COURAGE, HE SET HIMSELF UP AS A PROFESSIONAL BOUNTY HUNTER.
"DEAD OR ALIVE," THE POSTER SAID.
PROFITS WERE MODEST, AT FIRST...
HERE, VARMINT! YOU GET A FREE MEAL IN THE SALOON!
I.O.U. 1 meal Sheriff
HERE'S YER LUNCH, VARMINT!
4A
THEN, THE MONEY GOT BETTER...
AND BELT OPENED A BANK ACCOUNT.
I'M MAKING A LITTLE DEPOSIT.
HERE'S YER RECEIPT, VARMINT!
RECEIPT
ELLIOT BELT BECAME A BOUNTY HUNTER WITH A REPUTATION THAT WOULD MAKE A FIERCE APACHE WARRIOR SHAKE IN HIS MOCCASINS.
AND BY CHANCE, THE HUNT BROUGHT HIM TO CHEYENNE PASS.
SALOON · GILRS - WHISKEY · ICE COLD BEER
Morris + Goscinny
4B

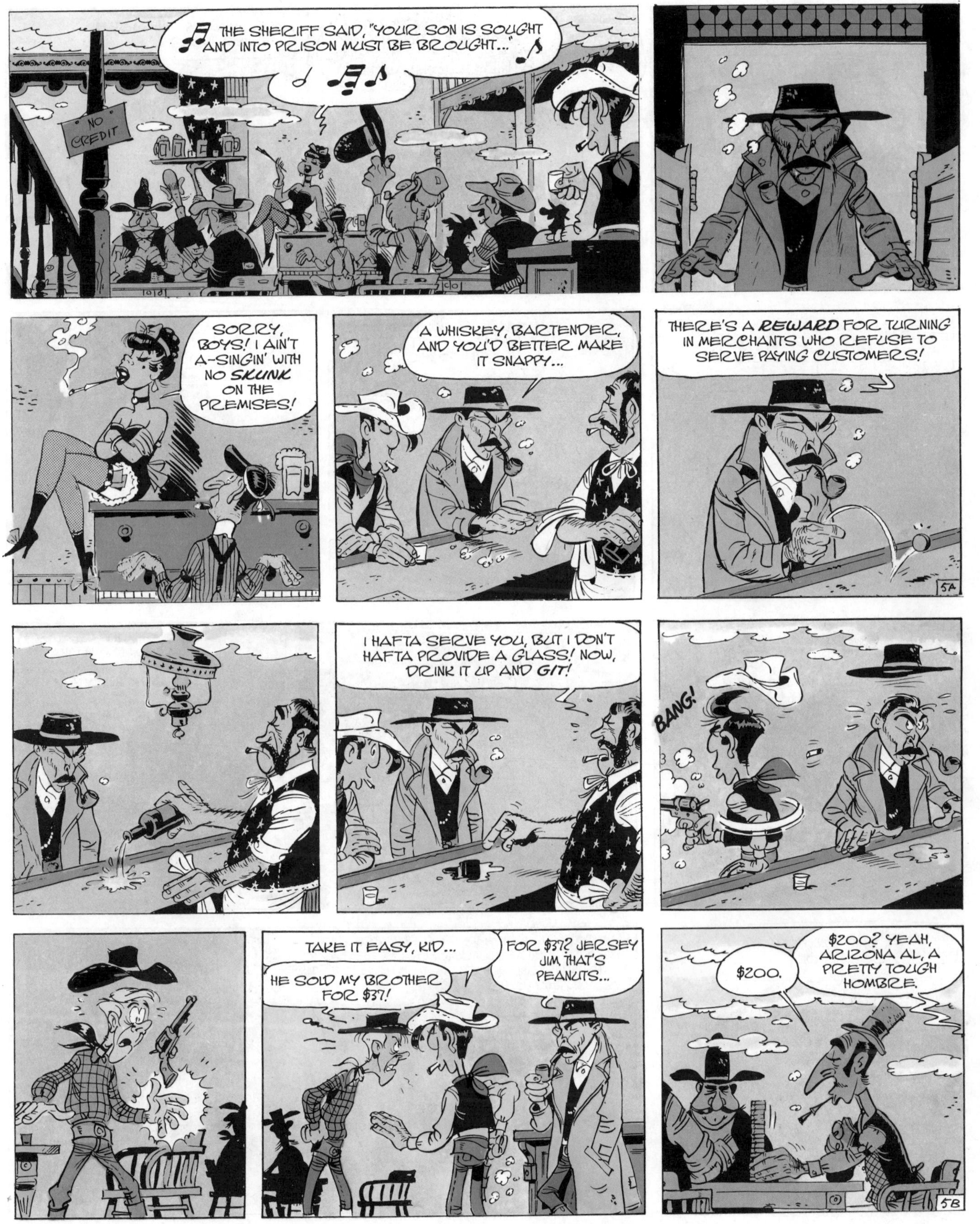
THE SHERIFF SAID, "YOUR SON IS SOUGHT AND INTO PRISON MUST BE BROUGHT..."
NO CREDIT
SORRY, BOYS! I AIN'T A-SINGIN' WITH NO SKUNK ON THE PREMISES!
A WHISKEY, BARTENDER, AND YOU'D BETTER MAKE IT SNAPPY...
THERE'S A REWARD FOR TURNING IN MERCHANTS WHO REFUSE TO SERVE PAYING CUSTOMERS!
I HAFTA SERVE YOU, BUT I DON'T HAFTA PROVIDE A GLASS! NOW, DRINK IT UP AND GIT!
BANG!
TAKE IT EASY, KID...
HE SOLD MY BROTHER FOR $37!
FOR $37? JERSEY JIM, THAT'S PEANUTS...
$200.
$200? YEAH, ARIZONA AL, A PRETTY TOUGH HOMBRE.

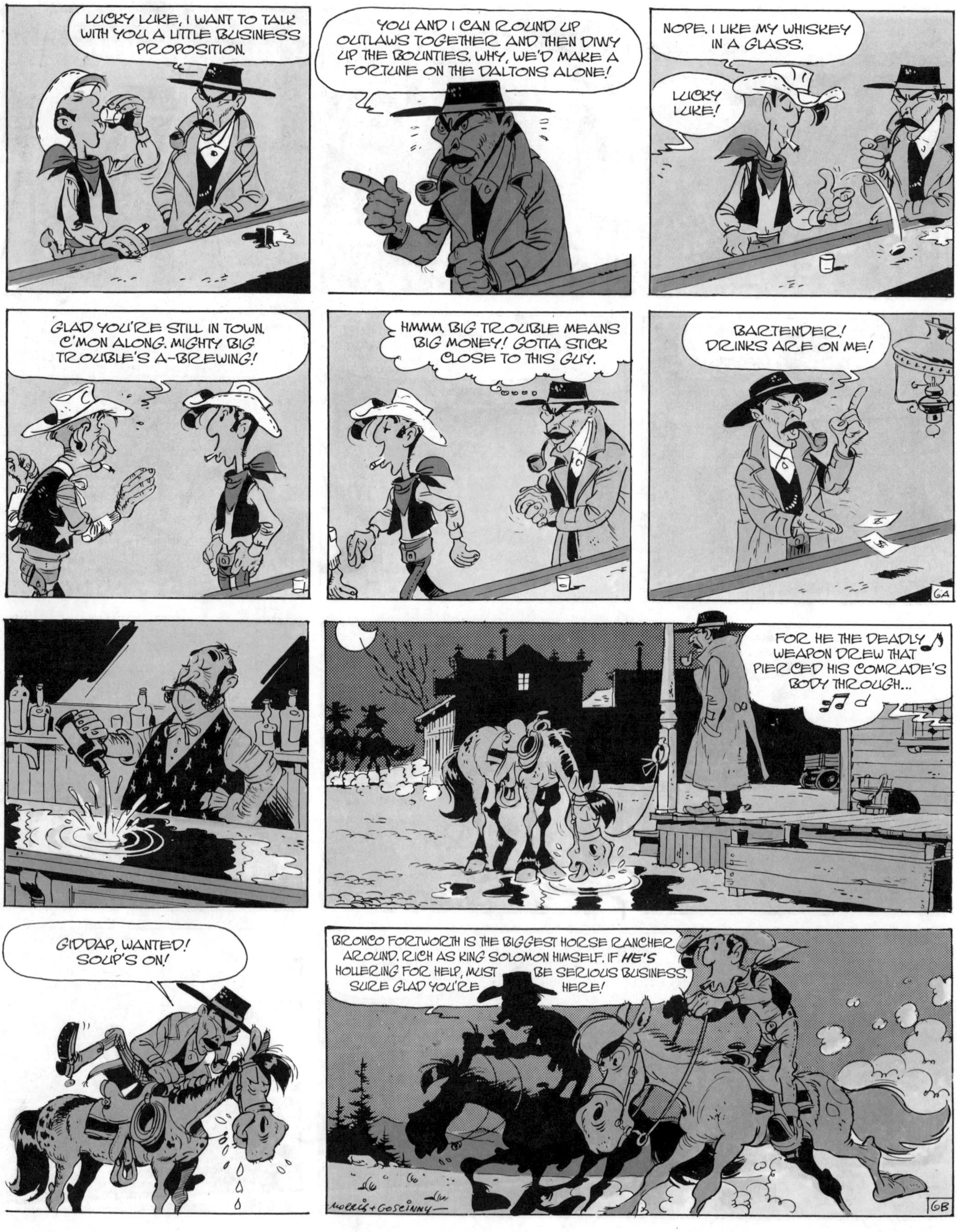
LUCKY LUKE, I WANT TO TALK WITH YOU. A LITTLE BUSINESS PROPOSITION.
YOU AND I CAN ROUND UP OUTLAWS TOGETHER AND THEN DIVY UP THE BOUNTIES. WHY, WE'D MAKE A FORTUNE ON THE DALTONS ALONE!
NOPE. I LIKE MY WHISKEY IN A GLASS.
LUCKY LUKE!
GLAD YOU'RE STILL IN TOWN. C'MON ALONG. MIGHTY BIG TROUBLE'S A-BREWING!
HMMM. BIG TROUBLE MEANS BIG MONEY! GOTTA STICK CLOSE TO THIS GUY.
BARTENDER! DRINKS ARE ON ME!
FOR HE THE DEADLY WEAPON DREW THAT PIERCED HIS COMRADE'S BODY THROUGH...
GIDDAP, WANTED! SOUP'S ON!
BRONCO FORTWORTH IS THE BIGGEST HORSE RANCHER AROUND. RICH AS KING SOLOMON HIMSELF. IF HE'S HOLLERING FOR HELP, MUST BE SERIOUS BUSINESS. SURE GLAD YOU'RE HERE!

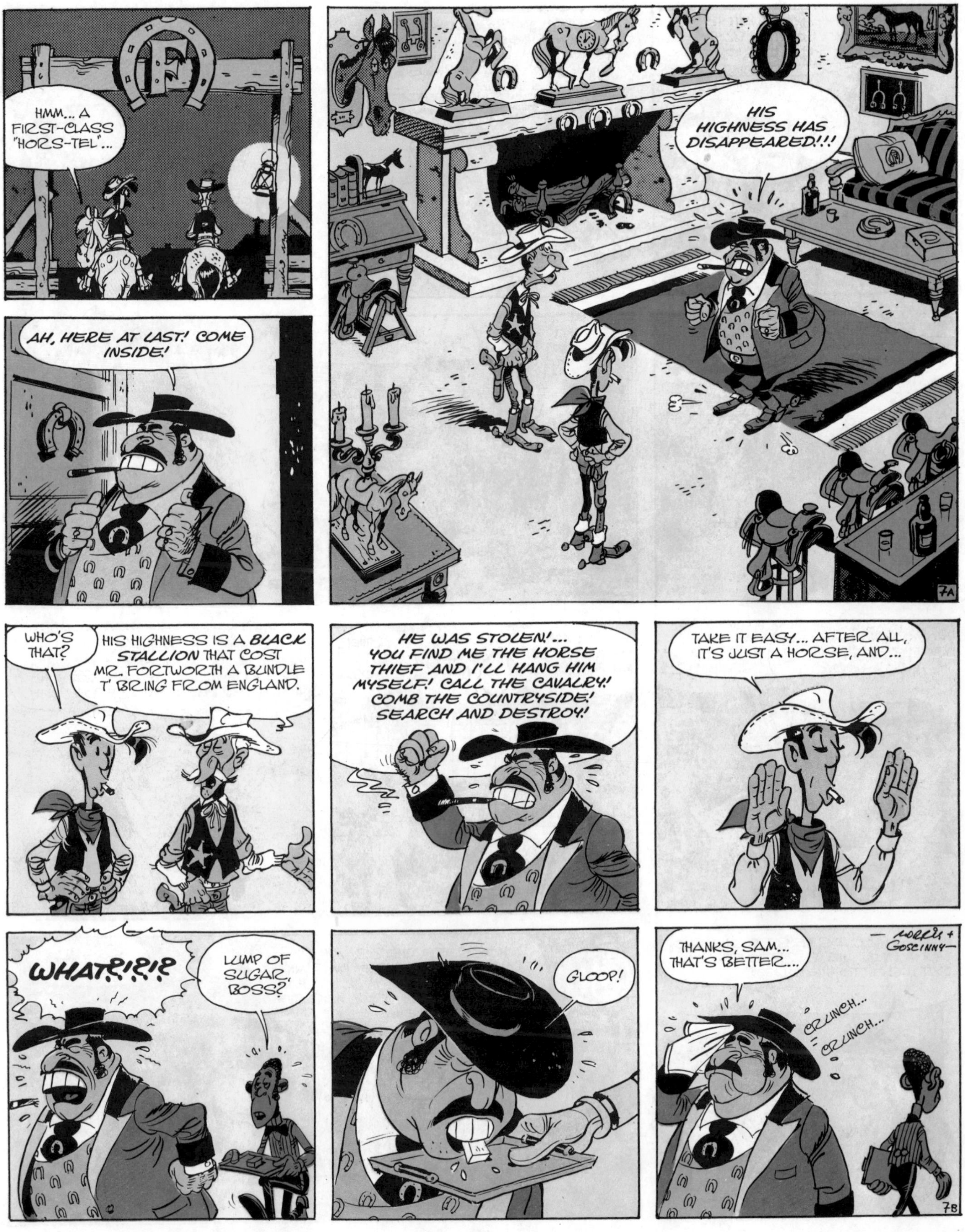
HMM... A FIRST-CLASS "HORS-TEL"...
AH, HERE AT LAST! COME INSIDE!
HIS HIGHNESS HAS DISAPPEARED!!!
WHO'S THAT?
HIS HIGHNESS IS A BLACK STALLION THAT COST MR. FORTWORTH A BUNDLE T' BRING FROM ENGLAND.
HE WAS STOLEN!... YOU FIND ME THE HORSE THIEF AND I'LL HANG HIM MYSELF! CALL THE CAVALRY! COMB THE COUNTRYSIDE! SEARCH AND DESTROY!
TAKE IT EASY... AFTER ALL, IT'S JUST A HORSE, AND...
WHAT?!?!?
LUMP OF SUGAR, BOSS?
GLOOP!
THANKS, SAM... THAT'S BETTER...
CRUNCH...
CRUNCH...

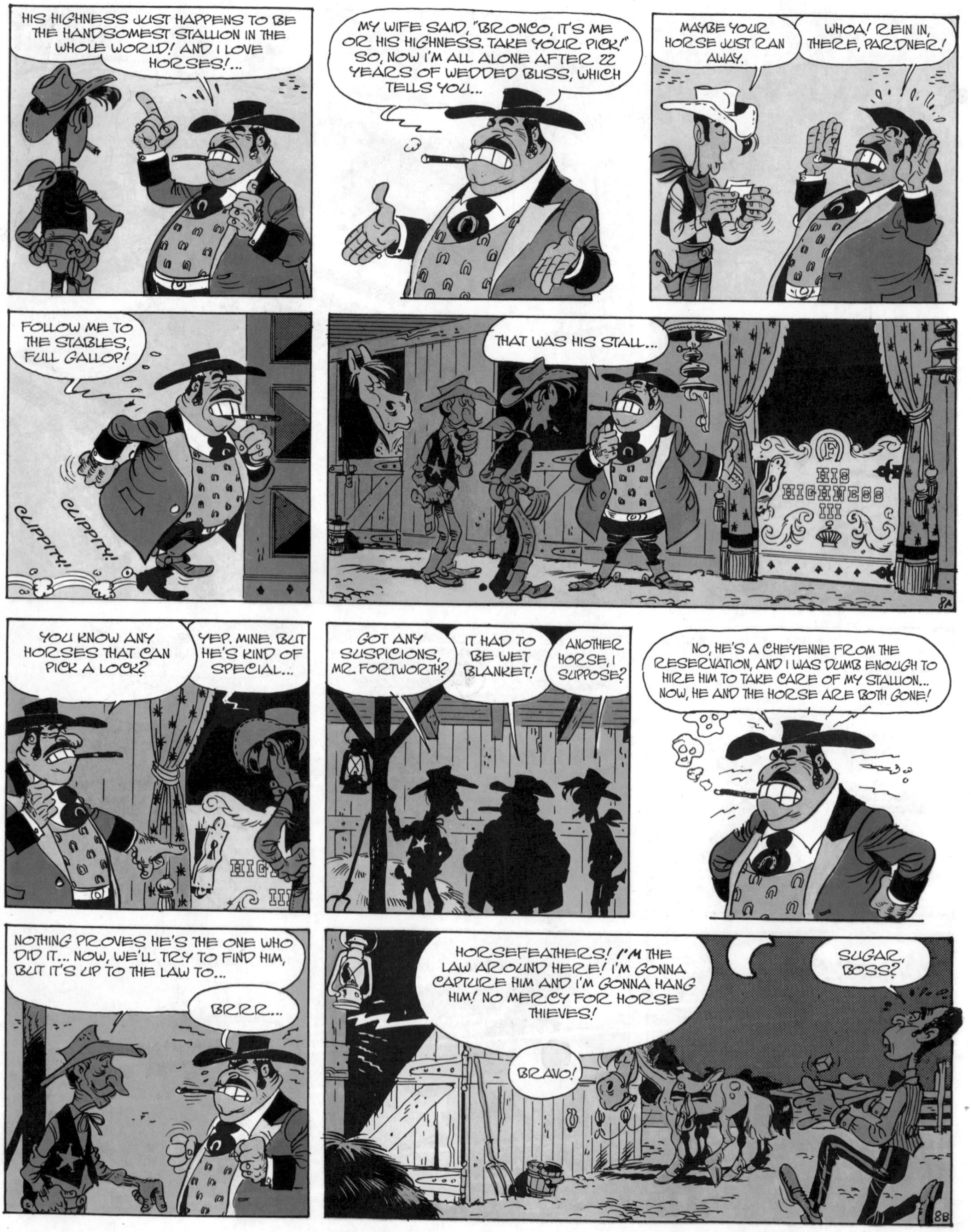
HIS HIGHNESS JUST HAPPENS TO BE THE HANDSOMEST STALLION IN THE WHOLE WORLD! AND I LOVE HORSES!...
MY WIFE SAID, "BRONCO, IT'S ME OR HIS HIGHNESS. TAKE YOUR PICK!" SO, NOW I'M ALL ALONE AFTER 22 YEARS OF WEDDED BLISS, WHICH TELLS YOU...
MAYBE YOUR HORSE JUST RAN AWAY.
WHOA! REIN IN, THERE, PARDNER!
FOLLOW ME TO THE STABLES, FULL GALLOP!
CLIPPITY!
CLIPPITY!
THAT WAS HIS STALL...
HIS HIGHNESS III
YOU KNOW ANY HORSES THAT CAN PICK A LOCK?
YEP. MINE. BUT HE'S KIND OF SPECIAL...
GOT ANY SUSPICIONS, MR. FORTWORTH?
IT HAD TO BE WET BLANKET!
ANOTHER HORSE, I SUPPOSE?
NO, HE'S A CHEYENNE FROM THE RESERVATION, AND I WAS DUMB ENOUGH TO HIRE HIM TO TAKE CARE OF MY STALLION... NOW, HE AND THE HORSE ARE BOTH GONE!
NOTHING PROVES HE'S THE ONE WHO DID IT... NOW, WE'LL TRY TO FIND HIM, BUT IT'S UP TO THE LAW TO...
BRRR...
HORSEFEATHERS! I'M THE LAW AROUND HERE! I'M GONNA CAPTURE HIM AND I'M GONNA HANG HIM! NO MERCY FOR HORSE THIEVES!
BRAVO!
SUGAR, BOSS?

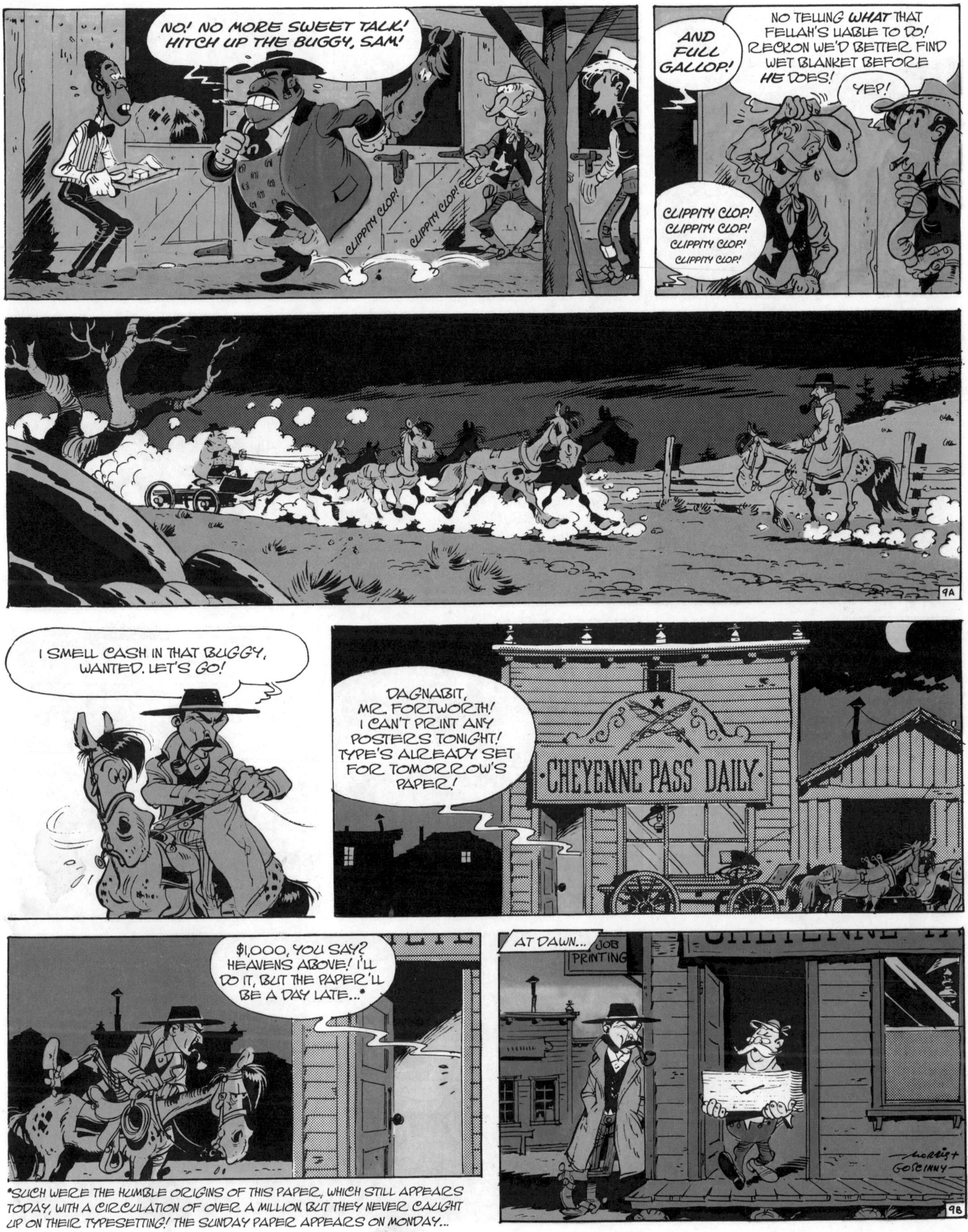
NO! NO MORE SWEET TALK! HITCH UP THE BUGGY, SAM!
CLIPPITY CLOP! CLIPPITY CLOP!
AND FULL GALLOP!
NO TELLING WHAT THAT FELLAH'S LIABLE TO DO! RECKON WE'D BETTER FIND WET BLANKET BEFORE HE DOES!
YEP!
CLIPPITY CLOP! CLIPPITY CLOP! CLIPPITY CLOP! CLIPPITY CLOP!
I SMELL CASH IN THAT BUGGY, WANTED. LET'S GO!
CHEYENNE PASS DAILY
DAGNABIT, MR. FORTWORTH! I CAN'T PRINT ANY POSTERS TONIGHT! TYPE'S ALREADY SET FOR TOMORROW'S PAPER!
$1,000, YOU SAY? HEAVENS ABOVE! I'LL DO IT, BUT THE PAPER'LL BE A DAY LATE...*
AT DAWN...
JOB PRINTING
MORRIS + GOSCINNY

*SUCH WERE THE HUMBLE ORIGINS OF THIS PAPER, WHICH STILL APPEARS TODAY, WITH A CIRCULATION OF OVER A MILLION. BUT THEY NEVER CAUGHT UP ON THEIR TYPESETTING! THE SUNDAY PAPER APPEARS ON MONDAY...

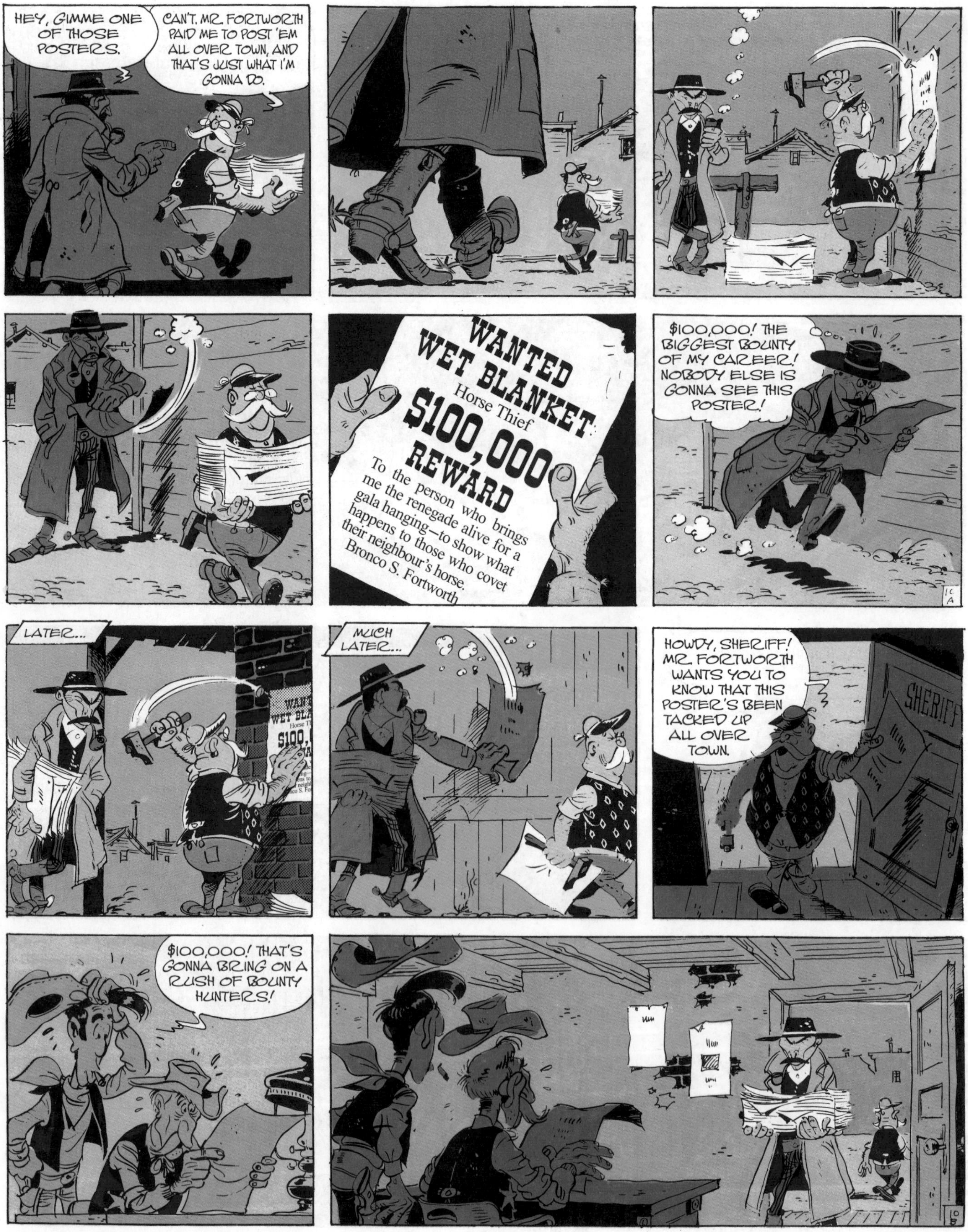
HEY, GIMME ONE OF THOSE POSTERS.
CAN'T. MR. FORTWORTH PAID ME TO POST 'EM ALL OVER TOWN, AND THAT'S JUST WHAT I'M GONNA DO.
WANTED
WET BLANKET
Horse Thief
$100,000
REWARD
To the person who brings me the renegade alive for a gala hanging—to show what happens to those who covet their neighbour's horse.
Bronco S. Fortworth
$100,000! THE BIGGEST BOUNTY OF MY CAREER! NOBODY ELSE IS GONNA SEE THIS POSTER!
LATER...
MUCH LATER...
HOWDY, SHERIFF! MR. FORTWORTH WANTS YOU TO KNOW THAT THIS POSTER'S BEEN TACKED UP ALL OVER TOWN.
SHERIFF
$100,000! THAT'S GONNA BRING ON A RUSH OF BOUNTY HUNTERS!

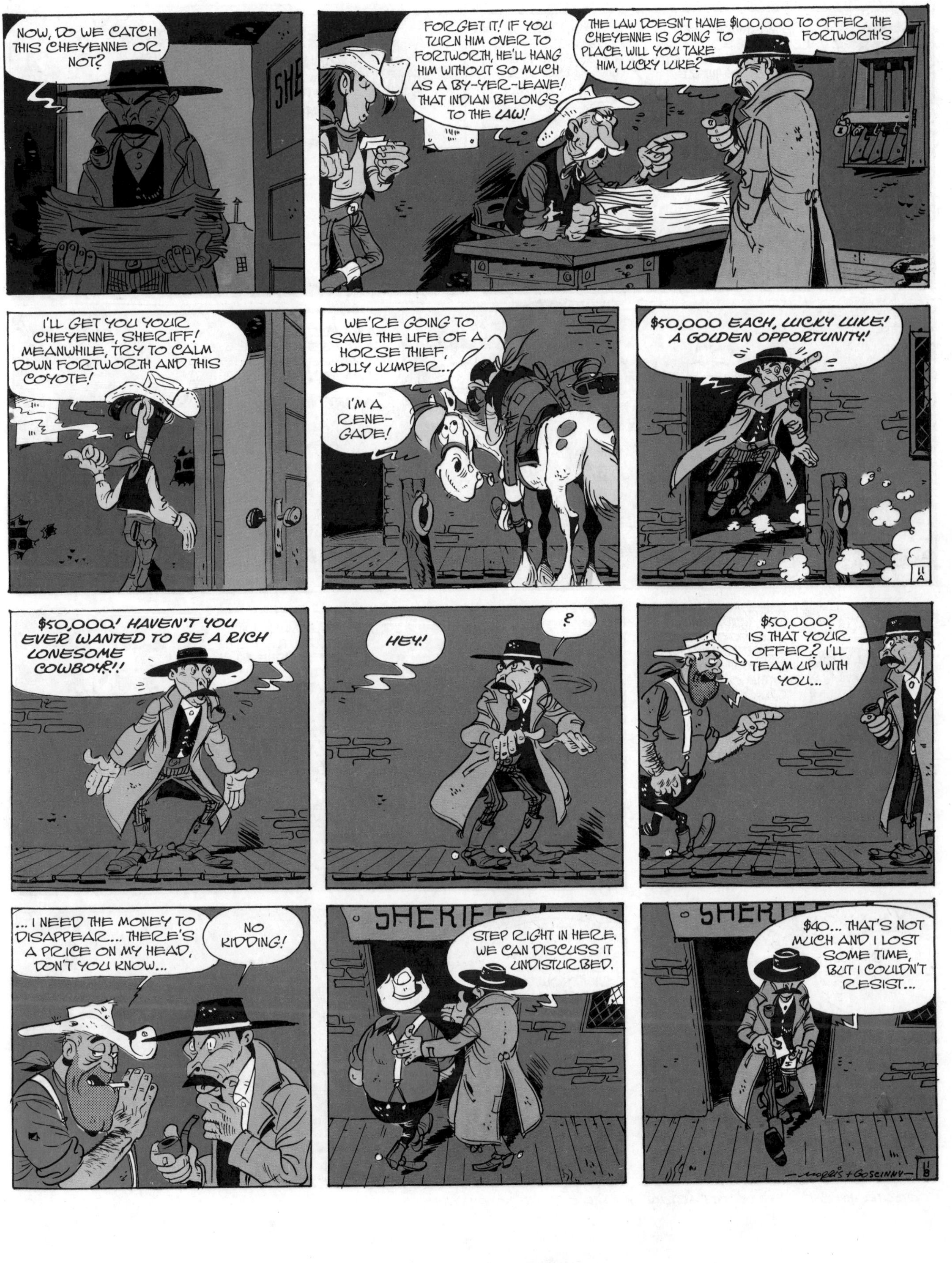
NOW, DO WE CATCH THIS CHEYENNE OR NOT?
FORGET IT! IF YOU TURN HIM OVER TO FORTWORTH, HE'LL HANG HIM WITHOUT SO MUCH AS A BY-YER-LEAVE! THAT INDIAN BELONGS TO THE LAW!
THE LAW DOESN'T HAVE $100,000 TO OFFER. THE CHEYENNE IS GOING TO FORTWORTH'S PLACE. WILL YOU TAKE HIM, LUCKY LUKE?
I'LL GET YOU YOUR CHEYENNE, SHERIFF! MEANWHILE, TRY TO CALM DOWN FORTWORTH AND THIS COYOTE!
WE'RE GOING TO SAVE THE LIFE OF A HORSE THIEF, JOLLY JUMPER...
I'M A RENE-GADE!
$50,000 EACH, LUCKY LUKE! A GOLDEN OPPORTUNITY!
$50,000! HAVEN'T YOU EVER WANTED TO BE A RICH LONESOME COWBOY?!!
HEY!
?
$50,000? IS THAT YOUR OFFER? I'LL TEAM UP WITH YOU...
... I NEED THE MONEY TO DISAPPEAR... THERE'S A PRICE ON MY HEAD, DON'T YOU KNOW...
NO KIDDING!
SHERIFF
STEP RIGHT IN HERE. WE CAN DISCUSS IT UNDISTURBED.
SHERIFF
$40... THAT'S NOT MUCH AND I LOST SOME TIME, BUT I COULDN'T RESIST...
MORRIS + GOSCINNY

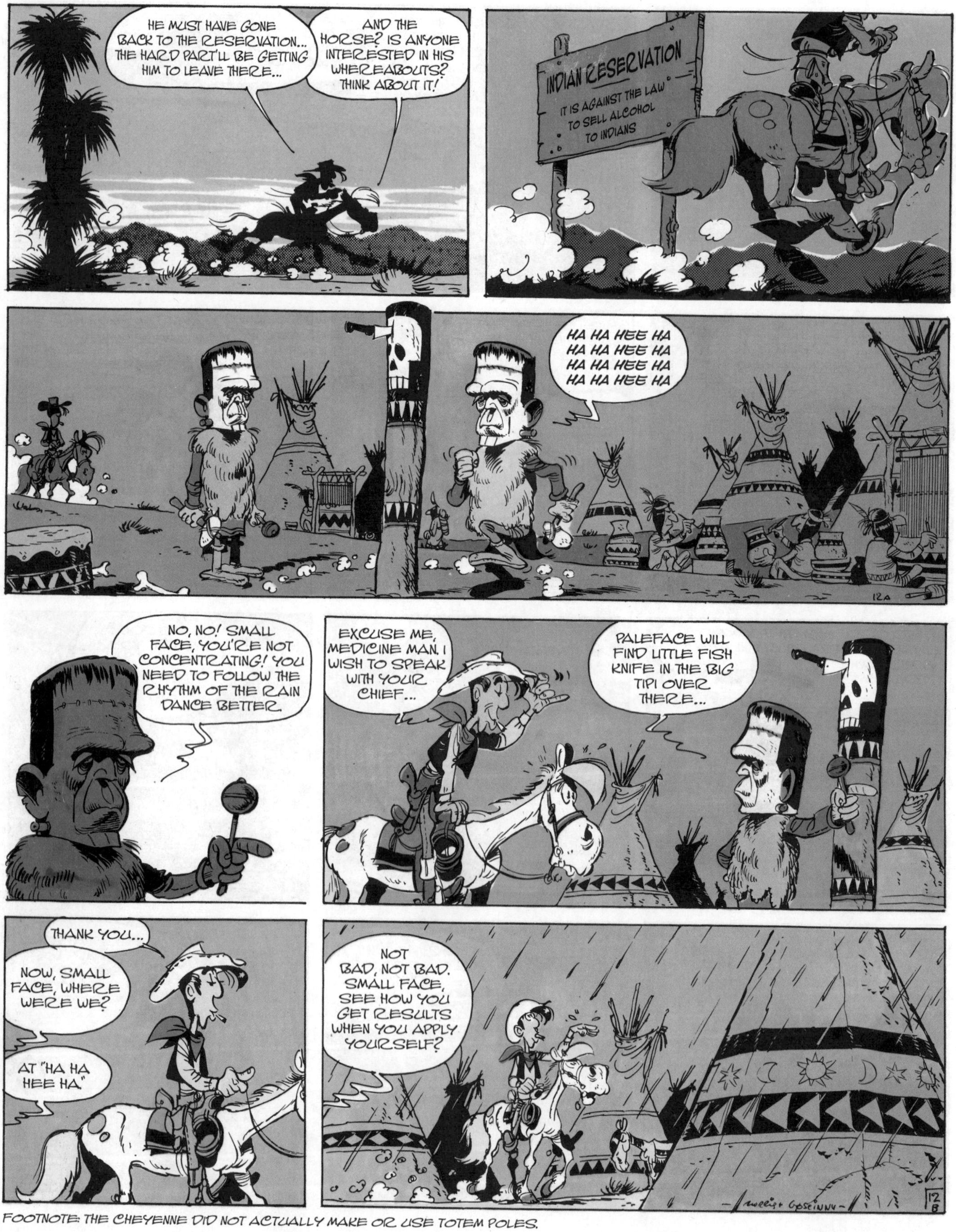
HE MUST HAVE GONE BACK TO THE RESERVATION... THE HARD PART'LL BE GETTING HIM TO LEAVE THERE...
AND THE HORSE? IS ANYONE INTERESTED IN HIS WHEREABOUTS? THINK ABOUT IT!
INDIAN RESERVATION
IT IS AGAINST THE LAW TO SELL ALCOHOL TO INDIANS
HA HA HEE HA HA HA HEE HA HA HA HEE HA HA HA HEE HA
NO, NO! SMALL FACE, YOU'RE NOT CONCENTRATING! YOU NEED TO FOLLOW THE RHYTHM OF THE RAIN DANCE BETTER.
EXCUSE ME, MEDICINE MAN. I WISH TO SPEAK WITH YOUR CHIEF...
PALEFACE WILL FIND LITTLE FISH KNIFE IN THE BIG TIPI OVER THERE...
THANK YOU...
NOW, SMALL FACE, WHERE WERE WE?
AT "HA HA HEE HA."
NOT BAD, NOT BAD. SMALL FACE, SEE HOW YOU GET RESULTS WHEN YOU APPLY YOURSELF?

FOOTNOTE: THE CHEYENNE DID NOT ACTUALLY MAKE OR USE TOTEM POLES.

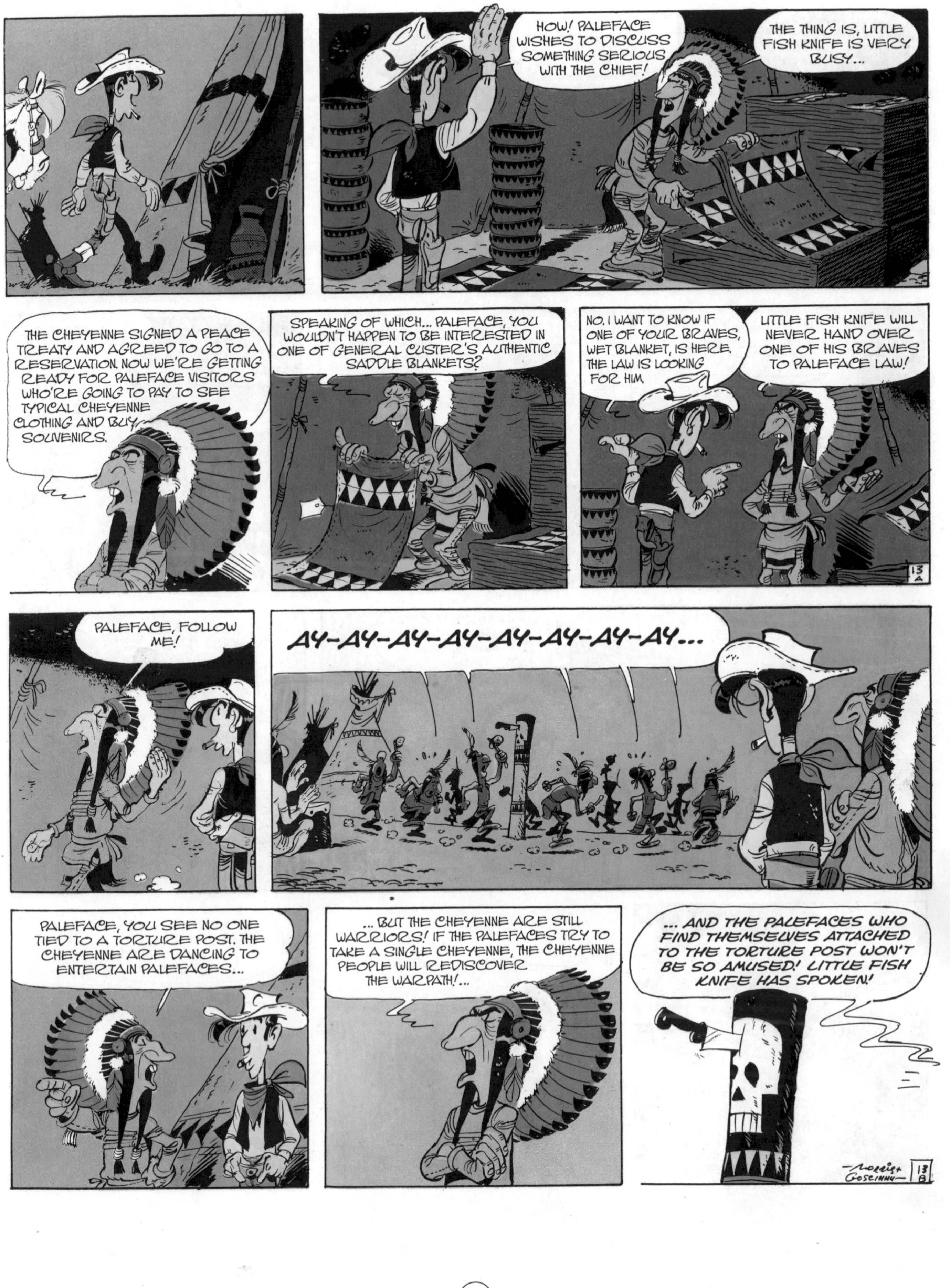

HOW! PALEFACE WISHES TO DISCUSS SOMETHING SERIOUS WITH THE CHIEF!
THE THING IS, LITTLE FISH KNIFE IS VERY BUSY...
THE CHEYENNE SIGNED A PEACE TREATY AND AGREED TO GO TO A RESERVATION. NOW WE'RE GETTING READY FOR PALEFACE VISITORS WHO'RE GOING TO PAY TO SEE TYPICAL CHEYENNE CLOTHING AND BUY SOUVENIRS.
SPEAKING OF WHICH... PALEFACE, YOU WOULDN'T HAPPEN TO BE INTERESTED IN ONE OF GENERAL CUSTER'S AUTHENTIC SADDLE BLANKETS?
NO. I WANT TO KNOW IF ONE OF YOUR BRAVES, WET BLANKET, IS HERE. THE LAW IS LOOKING FOR HIM.
LITTLE FISH KNIFE WILL NEVER HAND OVER ONE OF HIS BRAVES TO PALEFACE LAW!
13 A
PALEFACE, FOLLOW ME!
AY-AY-AY-AY-AY-AY-AY-AY...
PALEFACE, YOU SEE NO ONE TIED TO A TORTURE POST. THE CHEYENNE ARE DANCING TO ENTERTAIN PALEFACES...
... BUT THE CHEYENNE ARE STILL WARRIORS! IF THE PALEFACES TRY TO TAKE A SINGLE CHEYENNE, THE CHEYENNE PEOPLE WILL REDISCOVER THE WARPATH!...
... AND THE PALEFACES WHO FIND THEMSELVES ATTACHED TO THE TORTURE POST WON'T BE SO AMUSED! LITTLE FISH KNIFE HAS SPOKEN!
13 B

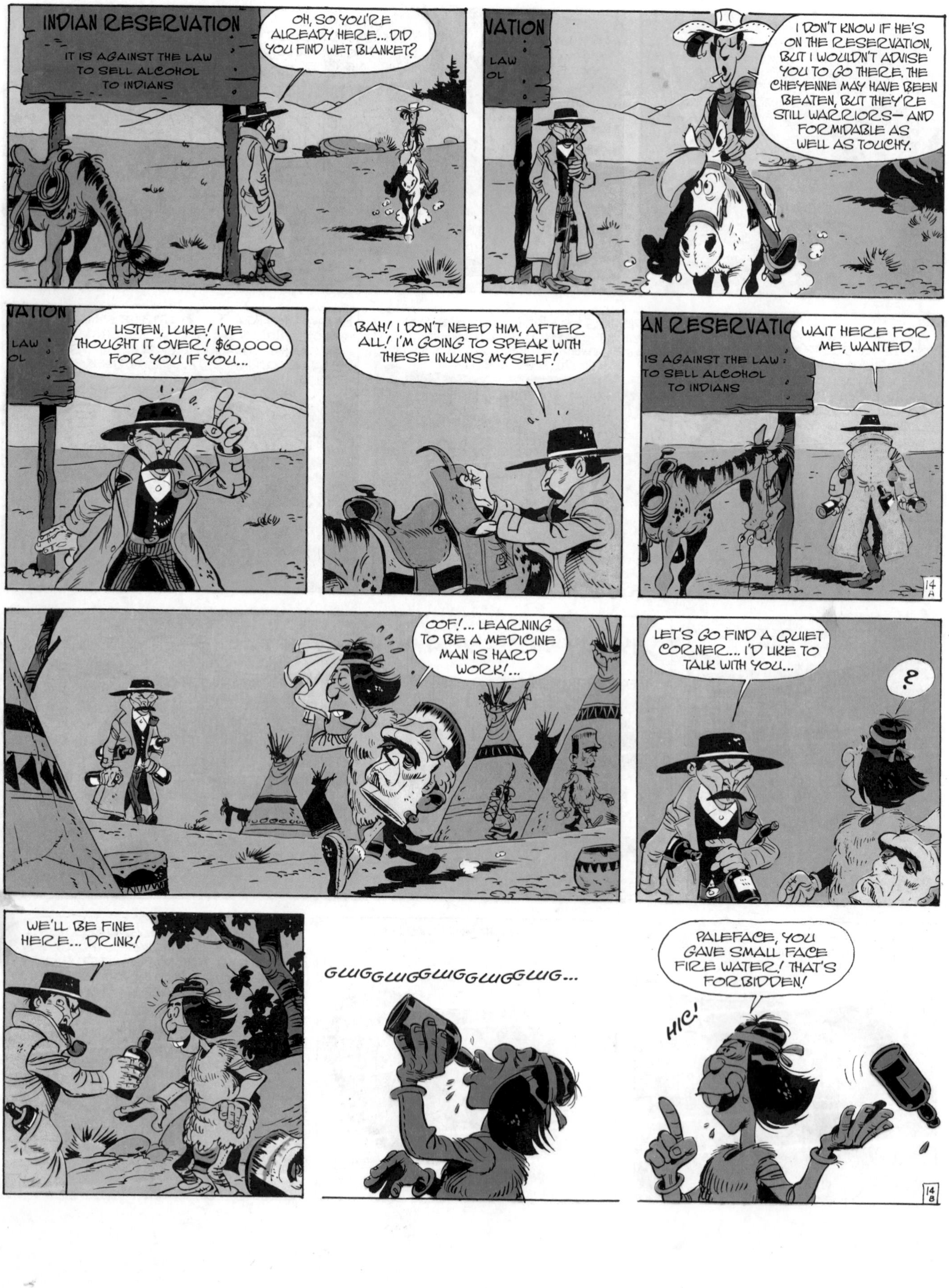
INDIAN RESERVATION
IT IS AGAINST THE LAW TO SELL ALCOHOL TO INDIANS
OH, SO YOU'RE ALREADY HERE... DID YOU FIND WET BLANKET?
I DON'T KNOW IF HE'S ON THE RESERVATION, BUT I WOULDN'T ADVISE YOU TO GO THERE. THE CHEYENNE MAY HAVE BEEN BEATEN, BUT THEY'RE STILL WARRIORS— AND FORMIDABLE AS WELL AS TOUCHY.
LISTEN, LUKE! I'VE THOUGHT IT OVER! $60,000 FOR YOU IF YOU...
BAH! I DON'T NEED HIM, AFTER ALL! I'M GOING TO SPEAK WITH THESE INJUNS MYSELF!
WAIT HERE FOR ME, WANTED.
OOF!... LEARNING TO BE A MEDICINE MAN IS HARD WORK!...
LET'S GO FIND A QUIET CORNER... I'D LIKE TO TALK WITH YOU...
?
WE'LL BE FINE HERE... DRINK!
GLUGGLUGGLUGGLUGGLUG...
HIC!
PALEFACE, YOU GAVE SMALL FACE FIRE WATER! THAT'S FORBIDDEN!

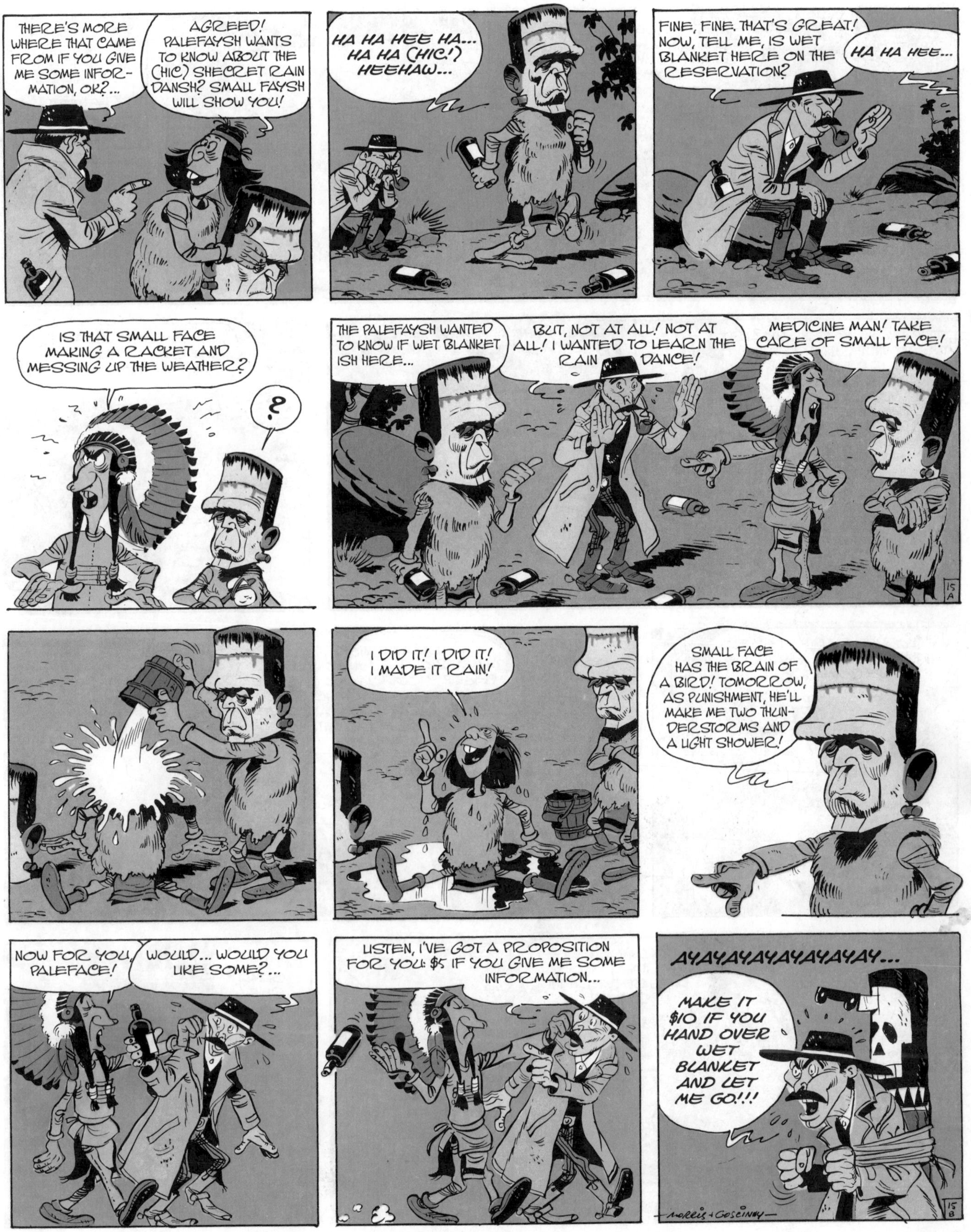

THERE'S MORE WHERE THAT CAME FROM IF YOU GIVE ME SOME INFORMATION, OK?...
AGREED! PALEFAYSH WANTS TO KNOW ABOUT THE (HIC) SHECRET RAIN DANSH? SMALL FAYSH WILL SHOW YOU!
HA HA HEE HA... HA HA (HIC!) HEEHAW...
FINE, FINE. THAT'S GREAT! NOW, TELL ME, IS WET BLANKET HERE ON THE RESERVATION?
HA HA HEE...
IS THAT SMALL FACE MAKING A RACKET AND MESSING UP THE WEATHER?
?
THE PALEFAYSH WANTED TO KNOW IF WET BLANKET ISH HERE...
BUT, NOT AT ALL! NOT AT ALL! I WANTED TO LEARN THE RAIN DANCE!
MEDICINE MAN! TAKE CARE OF SMALL FACE!
I DID IT! I DID IT! I MADE IT RAIN!
SMALL FACE HAS THE BRAIN OF A BIRD! TOMORROW, AS PUNISHMENT, HE'LL MAKE ME TWO THUNDERSTORMS AND A LIGHT SHOWER!
NOW FOR YOU, PALEFACE!
WOULD... WOULD YOU LIKE SOME?...
LISTEN, I'VE GOT A PROPOSITION FOR YOU: $5 IF YOU GIVE ME SOME INFORMATION...
AYAYAYAYAYAYAYAY...
MAKE IT $10 IF YOU HAND OVER WET BLANKET AND LET ME GO!!!
MORRIS + GOSCINNY

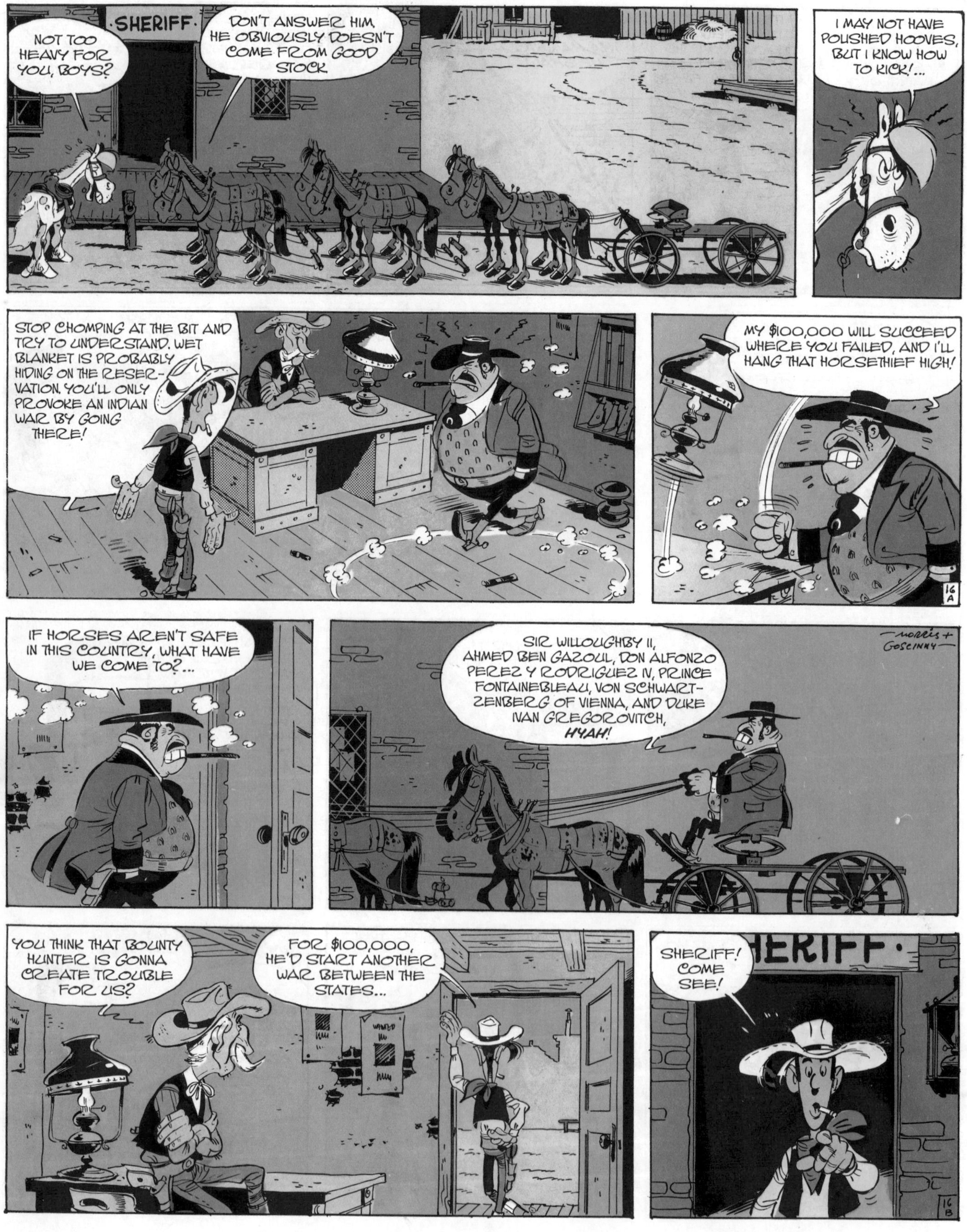
SHERIFF
NOT TOO HEAVY FOR YOU, BOYS?
DON'T ANSWER HIM, HE OBVIOUSLY DOESN'T COME FROM GOOD STOCK
I MAY NOT HAVE POLISHED HOOVES, BUT I KNOW HOW TO KICK!...
STOP CHOMPING AT THE BIT AND TRY TO UNDERSTAND. WET BLANKET IS PROBABLY HIDING ON THE RESERVATION. YOU'LL ONLY PROVOKE AN INDIAN WAR BY GOING THERE!
MY $100,000 WILL SUCCEED WHERE YOU FAILED, AND I'LL HANG THAT HORSETHIEF HIGH!
16 A
IF HORSES AREN'T SAFE IN THIS COUNTRY, WHAT HAVE WE COME TO?...
MORRIS + GOSCINNY
SIR WILLOUGHBY II, AHMED BEN GAZOUL, DON ALFONZO PEREZ Y RODRIGUEZ IV, PRINCE FONTAINEBLEAU, VON SCHWARTZENBERG OF VIENNA, AND DUKE IVAN GREGOROVITCH, HYAH!
YOU THINK THAT BOUNTY HUNTER IS GONNA CREATE TROUBLE FOR US?
FOR $100,000, HE'D START ANOTHER WAR BETWEEN THE STATES...
HERIFF
SHERIFF! COME SEE!
16 B

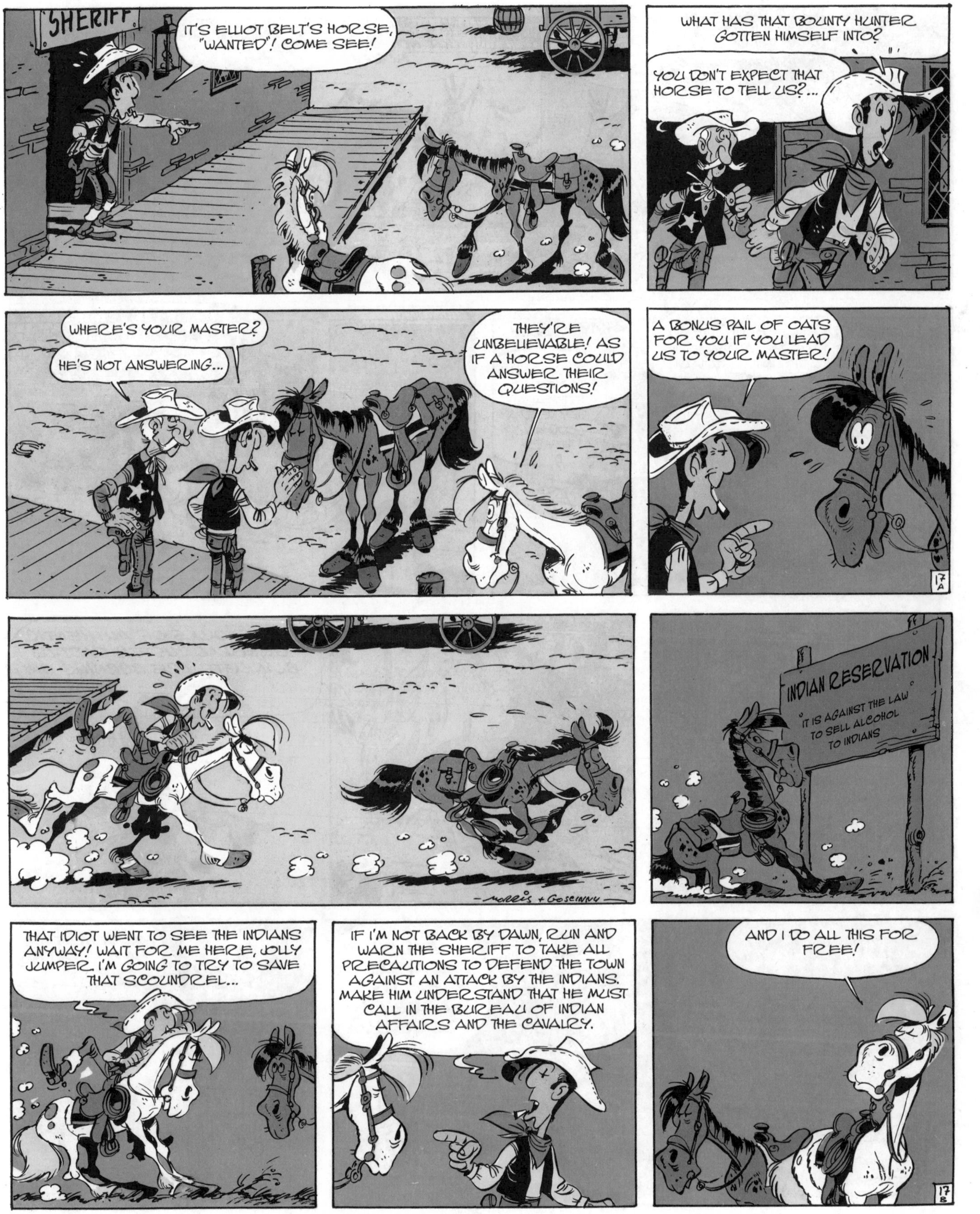
SHERIFF
IT'S ELLIOT BELT'S HORSE, "WANTED"! COME SEE!
WHAT HAS THAT BOUNTY HUNTER GOTTEN HIMSELF INTO?
YOU DON'T EXPECT THAT HORSE TO TELL US?...
WHERE'S YOUR MASTER?
HE'S NOT ANSWERING...
THEY'RE UNBELIEVABLE! AS IF A HORSE COULD ANSWER THEIR QUESTIONS!
A BONUS PAIL OF OATS FOR YOU IF YOU LEAD US TO YOUR MASTER!
INDIAN RESERVATION
IT IS AGAINST THE LAW TO SELL ALCOHOL TO INDIANS
MORRIS + GOSCINNY
THAT IDIOT WENT TO SEE THE INDIANS ANYWAY! WAIT FOR ME HERE, JOLLY JUMPER. I'M GOING TO TRY TO SAVE THAT SCOUNDREL...
IF I'M NOT BACK BY DAWN, RUN AND WARN THE SHERIFF TO TAKE ALL PRECAUTIONS TO DEFEND THE TOWN AGAINST AN ATTACK BY THE INDIANS. MAKE HIM UNDERSTAND THAT HE MUST CALL IN THE BUREAU OF INDIAN AFFAIRS AND THE CAVALRY.
AND I DO ALL THIS FOR FREE!

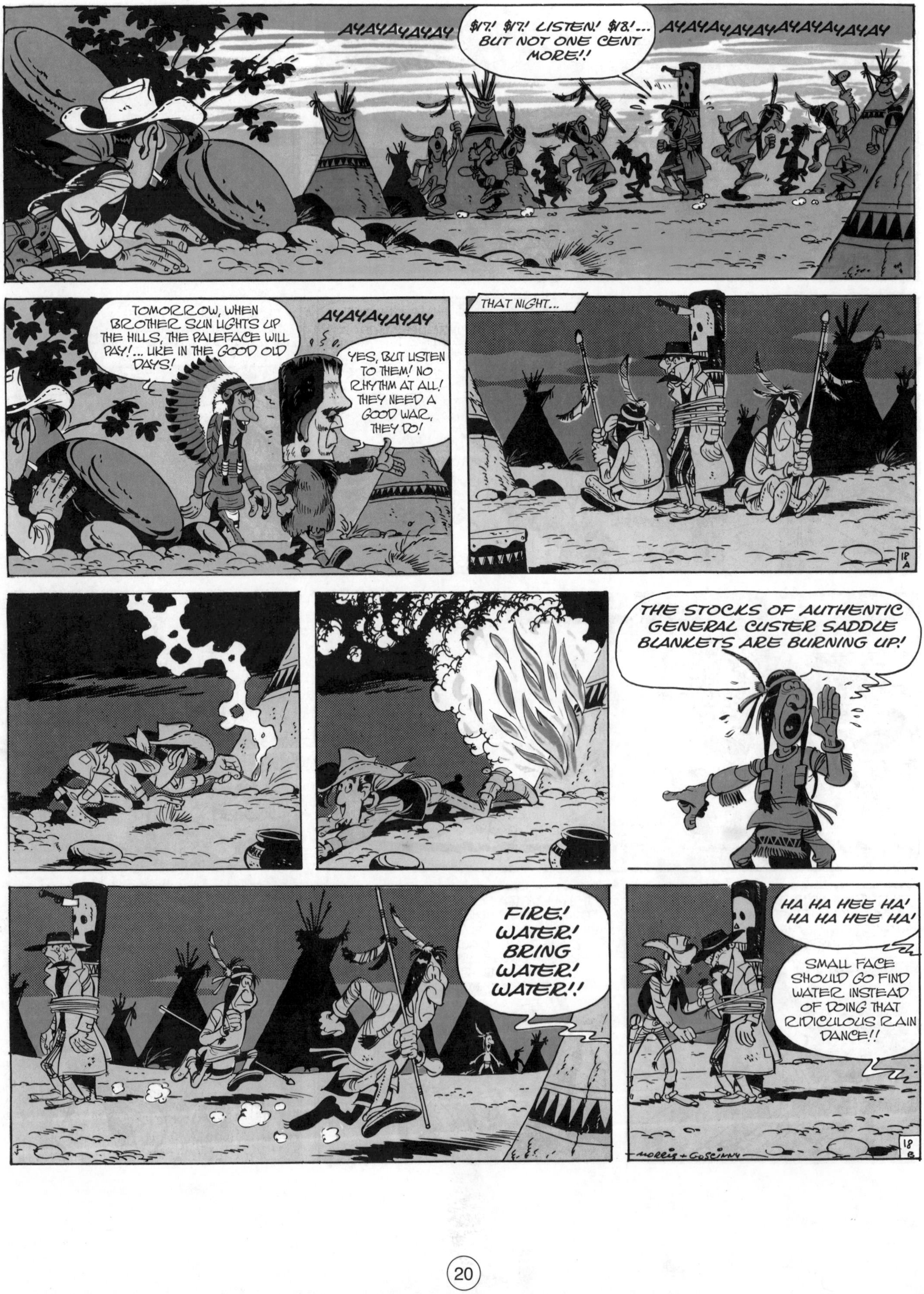

AYAYAYAYAY
$17! $17! LISTEN! $18!... BUT NOT ONE CENT MORE!!
AYAYAYAYAYAYAYAYAYAYAY
TOMORROW, WHEN BROTHER SUN LIGHTS UP THE HILLS, THE PALEFACE WILL PAY!... LIKE IN THE GOOD OLD DAYS!
AYAYAYAYAY
YES, BUT LISTEN TO THEM! NO RHYTHM AT ALL! THEY NEED A GOOD WAR, THEY DO!
THAT NIGHT...
18 A
THE STOCKS OF AUTHENTIC GENERAL CUSTER SADDLE BLANKETS ARE BURNING UP!
FIRE! WATER! BRING WATER! WATER!!
HA HA HEE HA! HA HA HEE HA!
SMALL FACE SHOULD GO FIND WATER INSTEAD OF DOING THAT RIDICULOUS RAIN DANCE!!
MORRIS + GOSCINNY
18 B

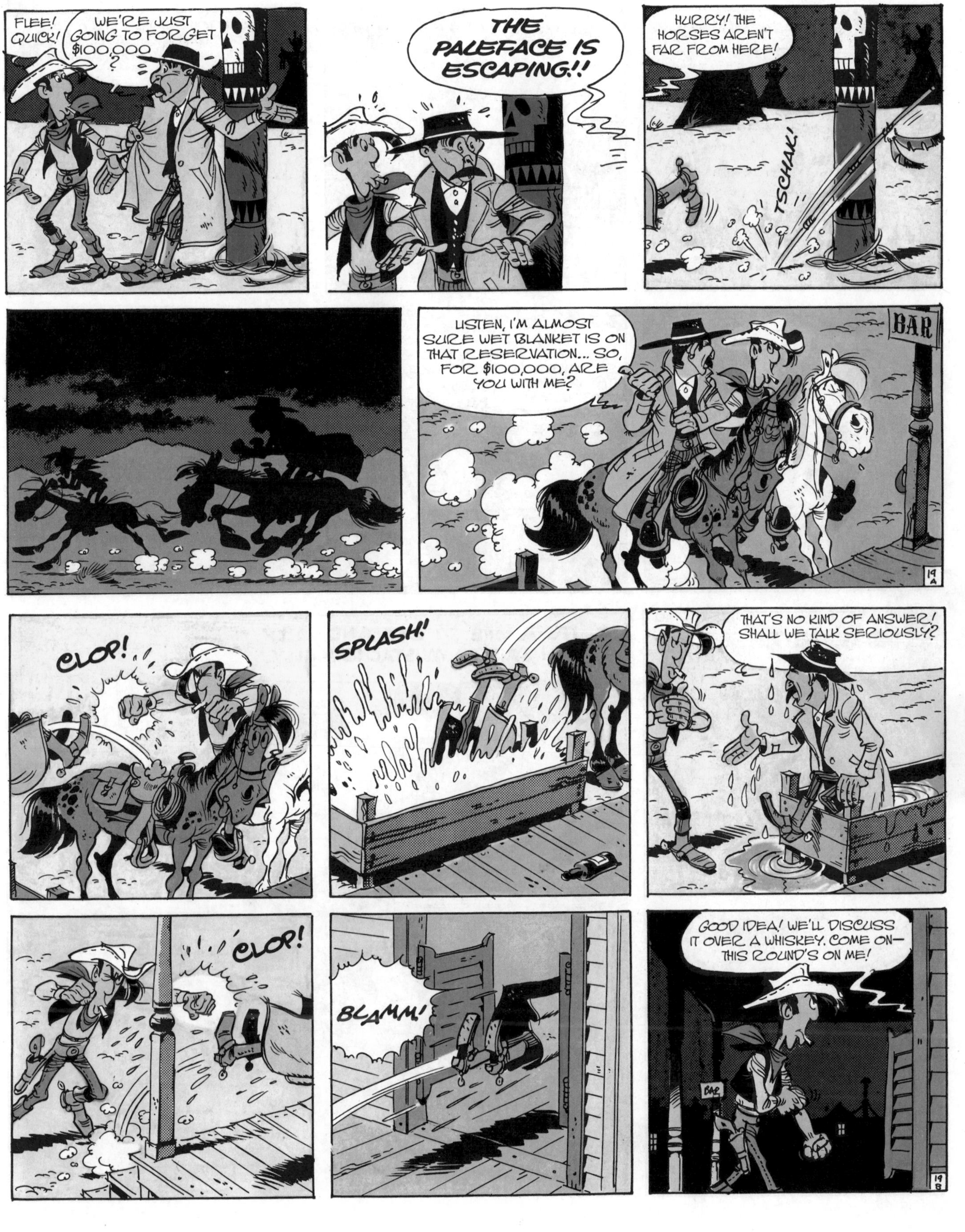
FLEE! QUICK!
WE'RE JUST GOING TO FORGET $100,000 ?
THE PALEFACE IS ESCAPING!!
HURRY! THE HORSES AREN'T FAR FROM HERE!
TSCHAK!
LISTEN, I'M ALMOST SURE WET BLANKET IS ON THAT RESERVATION... SO, FOR $100,000, ARE YOU WITH ME?
BAR
CLOP!
SPLASH!
THAT'S NO KIND OF ANSWER! SHALL WE TALK SERIOUSLY?
CLOP!
BLAMM!
GOOD IDEA! WE'LL DISCUSS IT OVER A WHISKEY. COME ON— THIS ROUND'S ON ME!
BAR

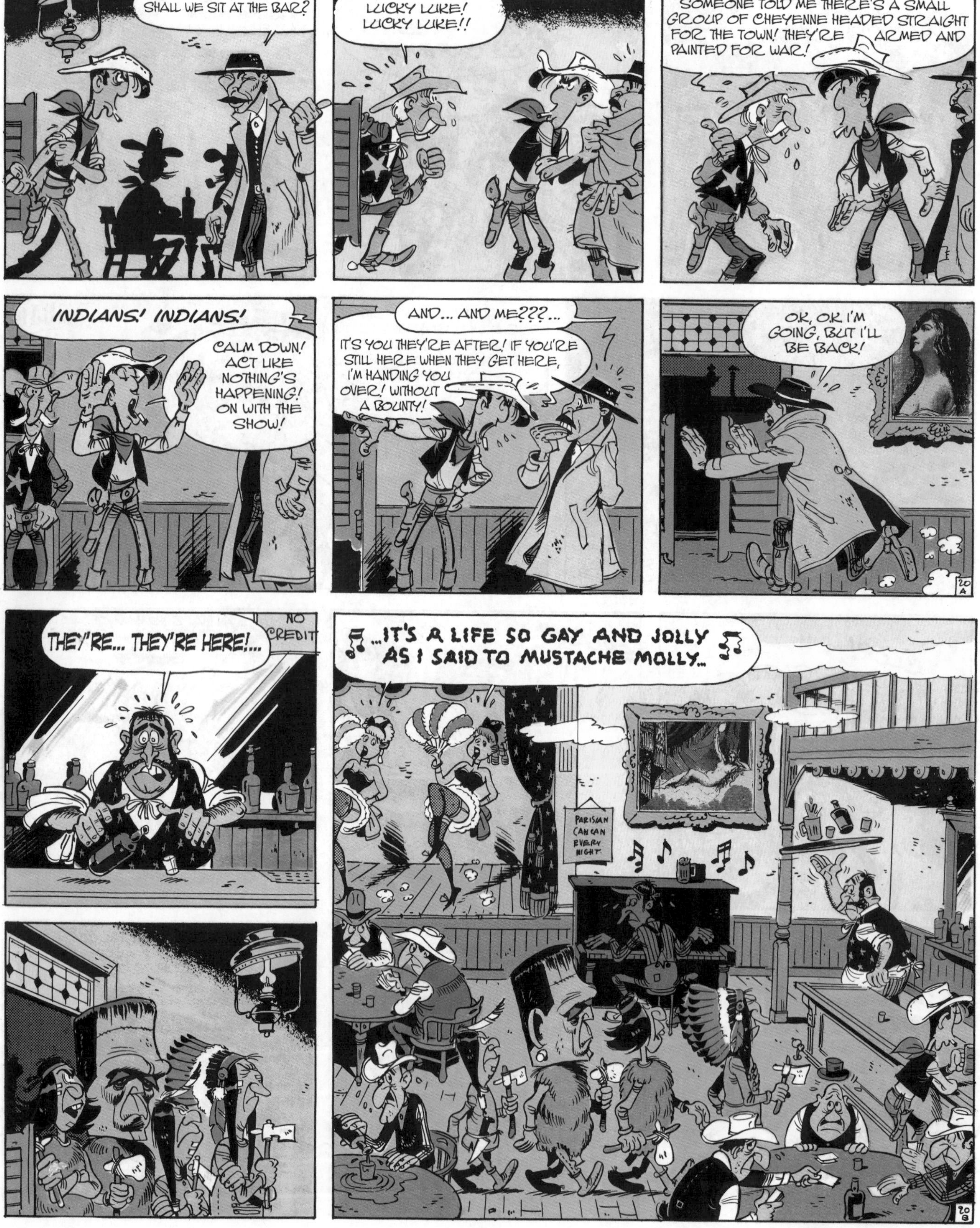
SHALL WE SIT AT THE BAR?
LUCKY LUKE! LUCKY LUKE!!
SOMEONE TOLD ME THERE'S A SMALL GROUP OF CHEYENNE HEADED STRAIGHT FOR THE TOWN! THEY'RE ARMED AND PAINTED FOR WAR!
INDIANS! INDIANS!
CALM DOWN! ACT LIKE NOTHING'S HAPPENING! ON WITH THE SHOW!
AND... AND ME???...
IT'S YOU THEY'RE AFTER! IF YOU'RE STILL HERE WHEN THEY GET HERE, I'M HANDING YOU OVER! WITHOUT A BOUNTY!
OK, OK I'M GOING, BUT I'LL BE BACK!
NO CREDIT
THEY'RE... THEY'RE HERE!...
...IT'S A LIFE SO GAY AND JOLLY AS I SAID TO MUSTACHE MOLLY...
PARISIAN CANCAN EVERY NIGHT

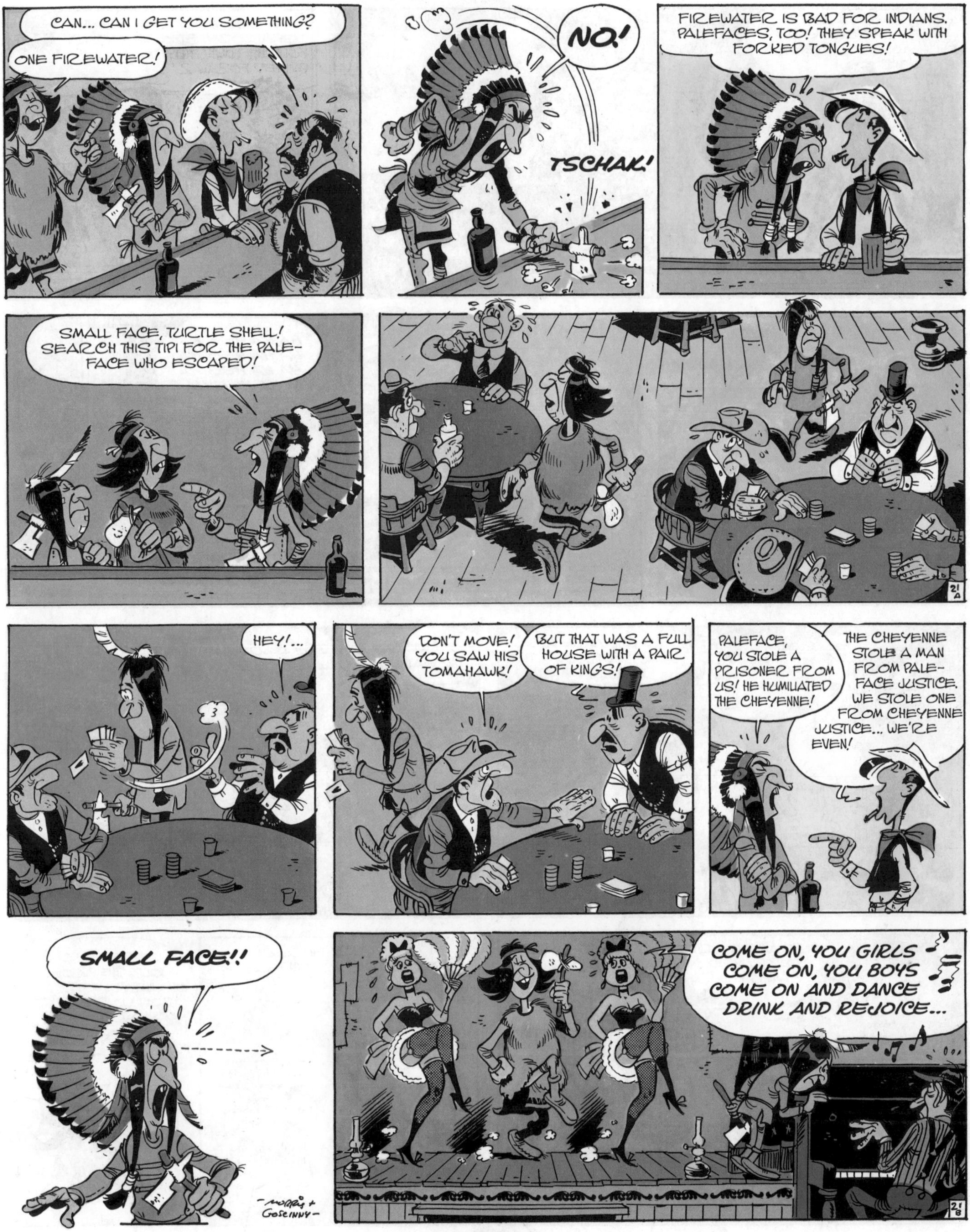
CAN... CAN I GET YOU SOMETHING?
ONE FIREWATER!
NO!
TSCHAK!
FIREWATER IS BAD FOR INDIANS. PALEFACES, TOO! THEY SPEAK WITH FORKED TONGUES!
SMALL FACE, TURTLE SHELL! SEARCH THIS TIPI FOR THE PALE-FACE WHO ESCAPED!
HEY!...
DON'T MOVE! YOU SAW HIS TOMAHAWK!
BUT THAT WAS A FULL HOUSE WITH A PAIR OF KINGS!
PALEFACE, YOU STOLE A PRISONER FROM US! HE HUMILIATED THE CHEYENNE!
THE CHEYENNE STOLE A MAN FROM PALE-FACE JUSTICE. WE STOLE ONE FROM CHEYENNE JUSTICE... WE'RE EVEN!
SMALL FACE!!
COME ON, YOU GIRLS
COME ON, YOU BOYS
COME ON AND DANCE
DRINK AND REJOICE...
MORRIS + GOSCINNY

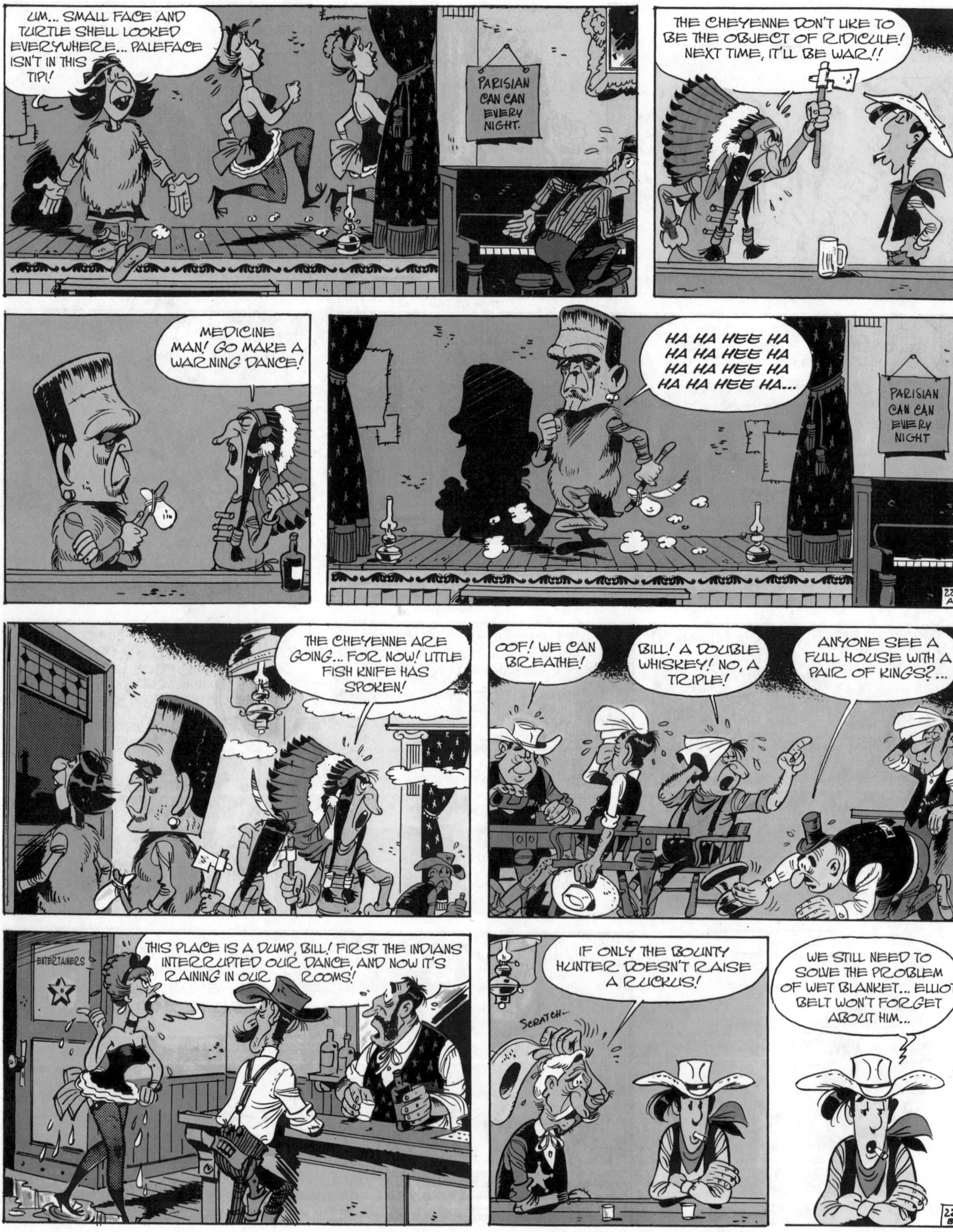
UM... SMALL FACE AND TURTLE SHELL LOOKED EVERYWHERE... PALEFACE ISN'T IN THIS TIPI!
PARISIAN CAN CAN EVERY NIGHT.
THE CHEYENNE DON'T LIKE TO BE THE OBJECT OF RIDICULE! NEXT TIME, IT'LL BE WAR!!
MEDICINE MAN! GO MAKE A WARNING DANCE!
HA HA HEE HA HA HA HEE HA HA HA HEE HA HA HA HEE HA...
PARISIAN CAN CAN EVERY NIGHT
22 A
THE CHEYENNE ARE GOING... FOR NOW! LITTLE FISH KNIFE HAS SPOKEN!
OOF! WE CAN BREATHE!
BILL! A DOUBLE WHISKEY! NO, A TRIPLE!
ANYONE SEE A FULL HOUSE WITH A PAIR OF KINGS?...
ENTERTAINERS
THIS PLACE IS A DUMP, BILL! FIRST THE INDIANS INTERRUPTED OUR DANCE, AND NOW IT'S RAINING IN OUR ROOMS!
IF ONLY THE BOUNTY HUNTER DOESN'T RAISE A RUCKUS!
SCRATCH...
WE STILL NEED TO SOLVE THE PROBLEM OF WET BLANKET... ELLIOT BELT WON'T FORGET ABOUT HIM...
22 B

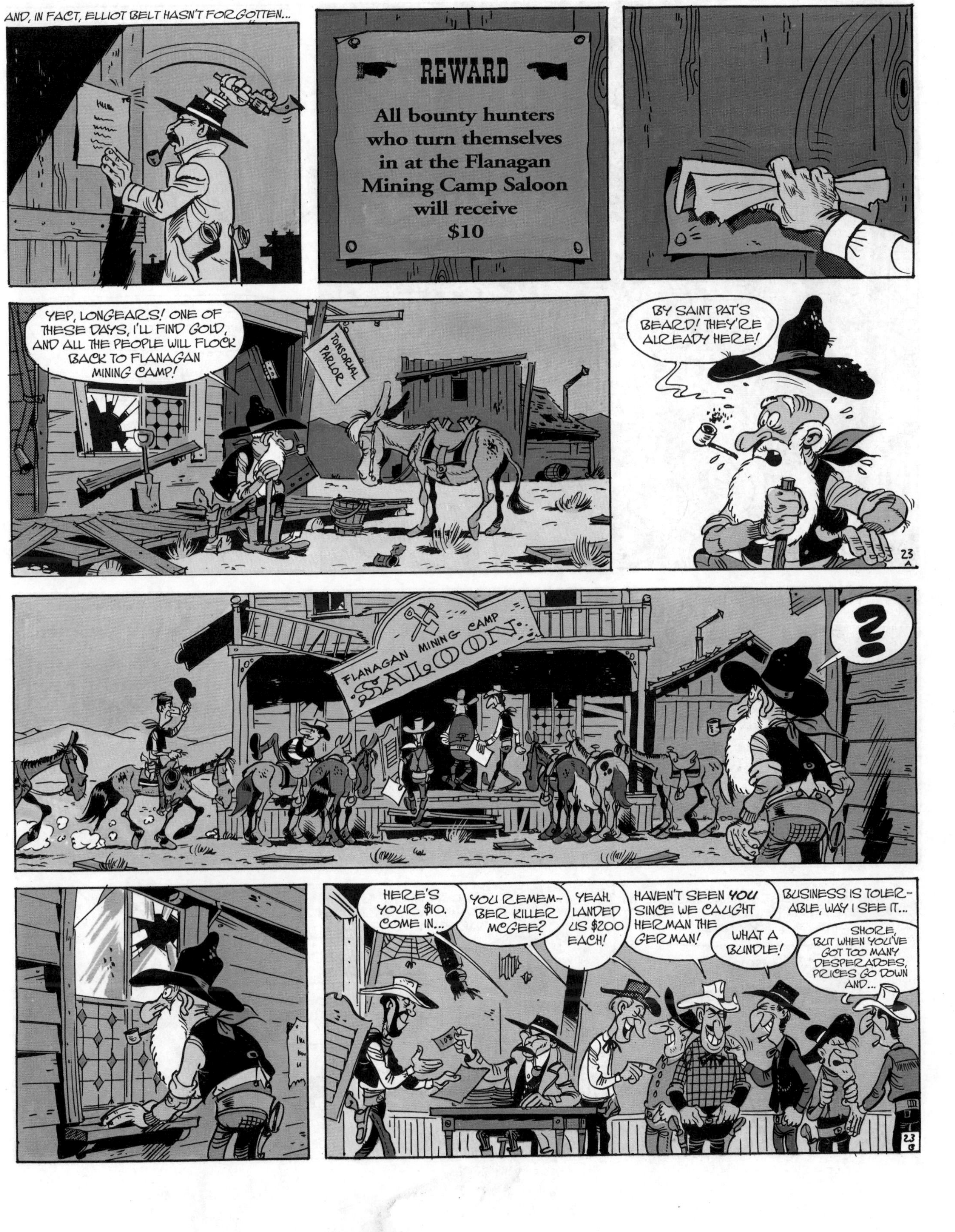
AND, IN FACT, ELLIOT BELT HASN'T FORGOTTEN...
REWARD
All bounty hunters who turn themselves in at the Flanagan Mining Camp Saloon will receive $10
YEP, LONGEARS! ONE OF THESE DAYS, I'LL FIND GOLD, AND ALL THE PEOPLE WILL FLOCK BACK TO FLANAGAN MINING CAMP!
TONSORIAL PARLOR
BY SAINT PAT'S BEARD! THEY'RE ALREADY HERE!
FLANAGAN MINING CAMP SALOON
?
HERE'S YOUR $10. COME IN...
YOU REMEMBER KILLER McGEE?
YEAH. LANDED US $200 EACH!
HAVEN'T SEEN YOU SINCE WE CAUGHT HERMAN THE GERMAN!
WHAT A BUNDLE!
BUSINESS IS TOLERABLE, WAY I SEE IT...
SHORE, BUT WHEN YOU'VE GOT TOO MANY DESPERADOES, PRICES GO DOWN AND...

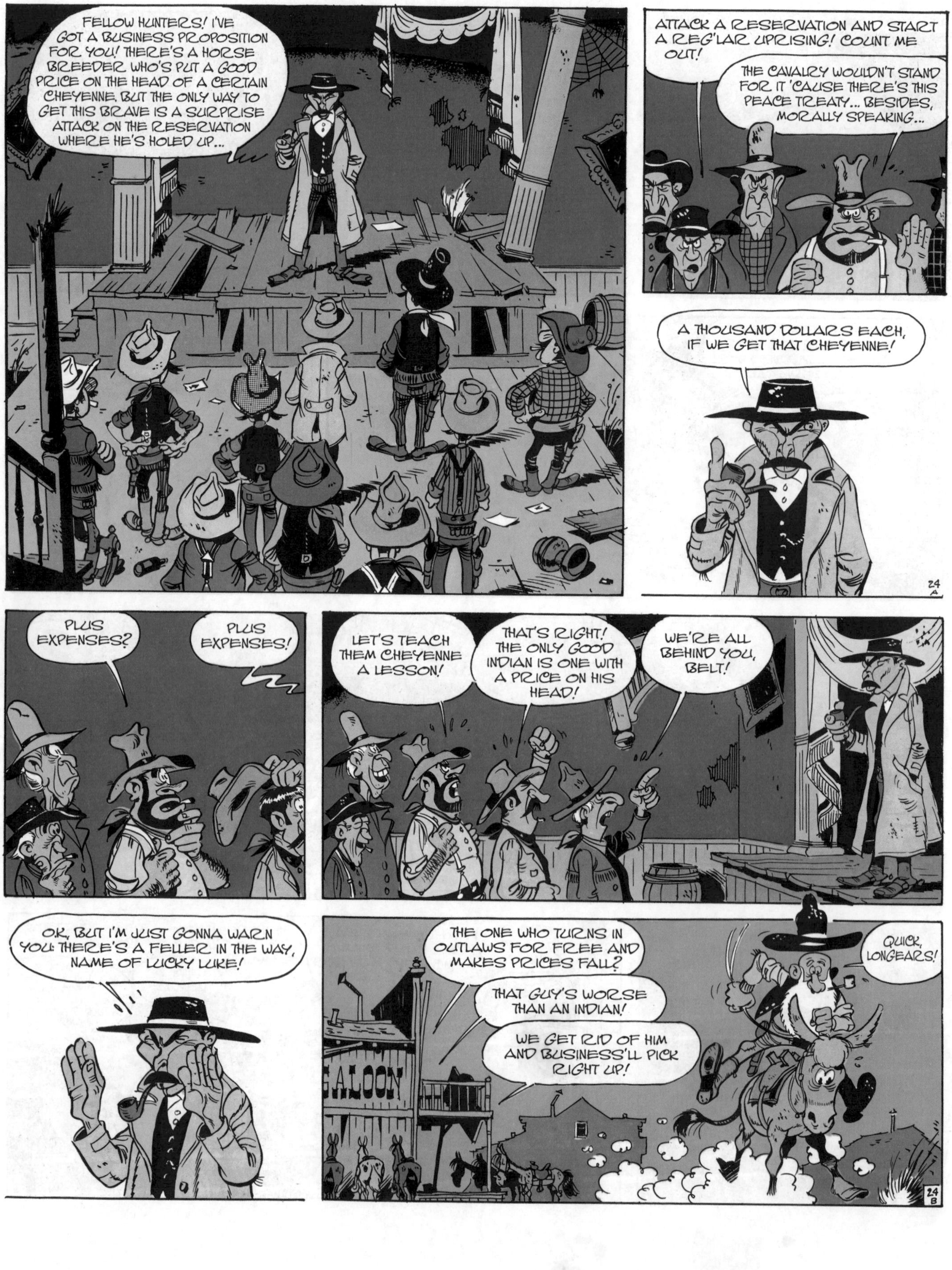
FELLOW HUNTERS! I'VE GOT A BUSINESS PROPOSITION FOR YOU! THERE'S A HORSE BREEDER WHO'S PUT A GOOD PRICE ON THE HEAD OF A CERTAIN CHEYENNE, BUT THE ONLY WAY TO GET THIS BRAVE IS A SURPRISE ATTACK ON THE RESERVATION WHERE HE'S HOLED UP...
ATTACK A RESERVATION AND START A REG'LAR UPRISING! COUNT ME OUT!
THE CAVALRY WOULDN'T STAND FOR IT 'CAUSE THERE'S THIS PEACE TREATY... BESIDES, MORALLY SPEAKING...
A THOUSAND DOLLARS EACH, IF WE GET THAT CHEYENNE!
PLUS EXPENSES?
PLUS EXPENSES!
LET'S TEACH THEM CHEYENNE A LESSON!
THAT'S RIGHT! THE ONLY GOOD INDIAN IS ONE WITH A PRICE ON HIS HEAD!
WE'RE ALL BEHIND YOU, BELT!
OK, BUT I'M JUST GONNA WARN YOU: THERE'S A FELLER IN THE WAY, NAME OF LUCKY LUKE!
THE ONE WHO TURNS IN OUTLAWS FOR FREE AND MAKES PRICES FALL?
THAT GUY'S WORSE THAN AN INDIAN!
WE GET RID OF HIM AND BUSINESS'LL PICK RIGHT UP!
QUICK, LONGEARS!
SALOON

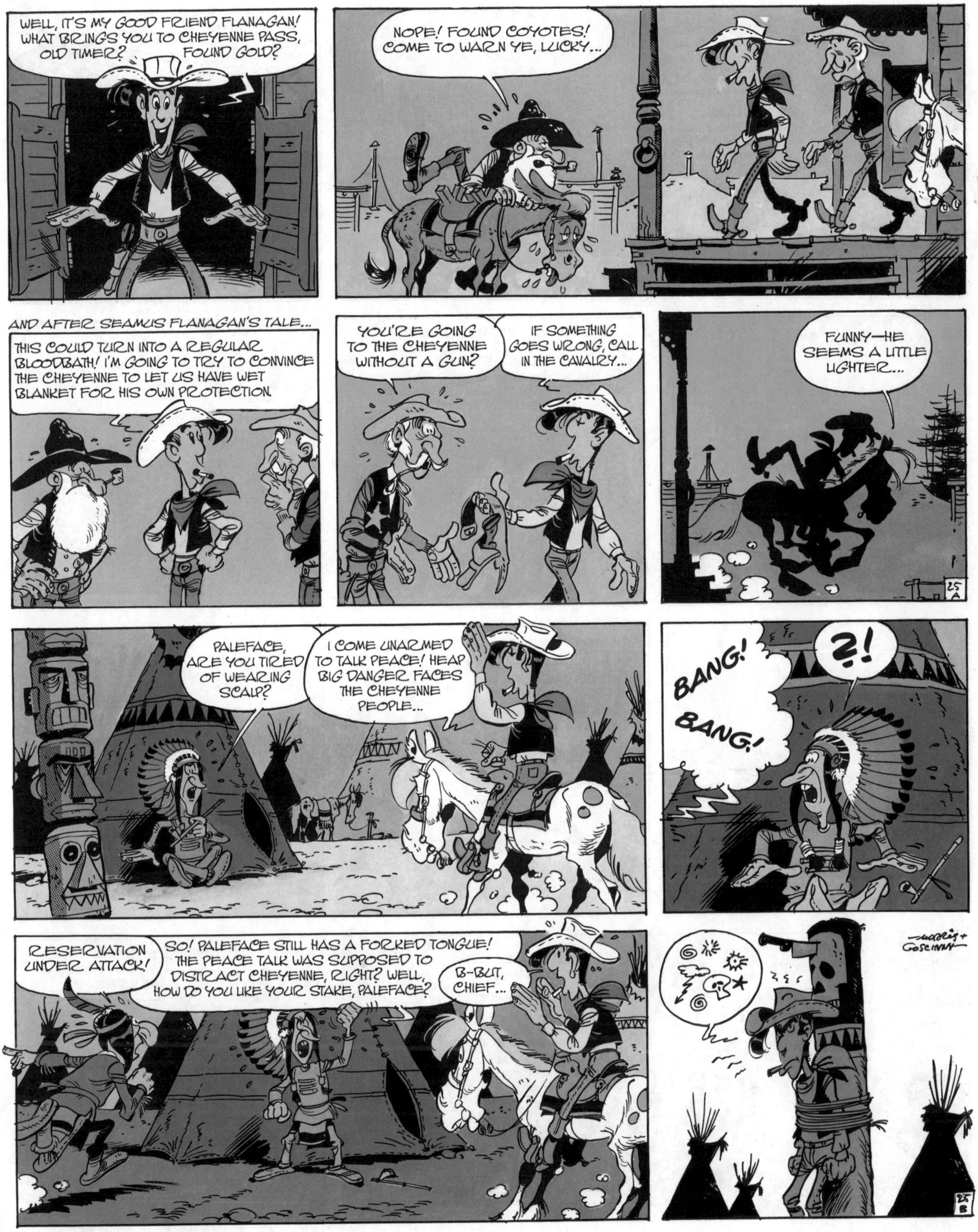
WELL, IT'S MY GOOD FRIEND FLANAGAN! WHAT BRINGS YOU TO CHEYENNE PASS, OLD TIMER? FOUND GOLD?
NOPE! FOUND COYOTES! COME TO WARN YE, LUCKY...
AND AFTER SEAMUS FLANAGAN'S TALE...
THIS COULD TURN INTO A REGULAR BLOODBATH! I'M GOING TO TRY TO CONVINCE THE CHEYENNE TO LET US HAVE WET BLANKET FOR HIS OWN PROTECTION.
YOU'RE GOING TO THE CHEYENNE WITHOUT A GUN?
IF SOMETHING GOES WRONG, CALL IN THE CAVALRY...
FUNNY—HE SEEMS A LITTLE LIGHTER...
PALEFACE, ARE YOU TIRED OF WEARING SCALP?
I COME UNARMED TO TALK PEACE! HEAP BIG DANGER FACES THE CHEYENNE PEOPLE...
BANG!
BANG!
?!
RESERVATION UNDER ATTACK!
SO! PALEFACE STILL HAS A FORKED TONGUE! THE PEACE TALK WAS SUPPOSED TO DISTRACT CHEYENNE, RIGHT? WELL, HOW DO YOU LIKE YOUR STAKE, PALEFACE?
B-BUT, CHIEF...

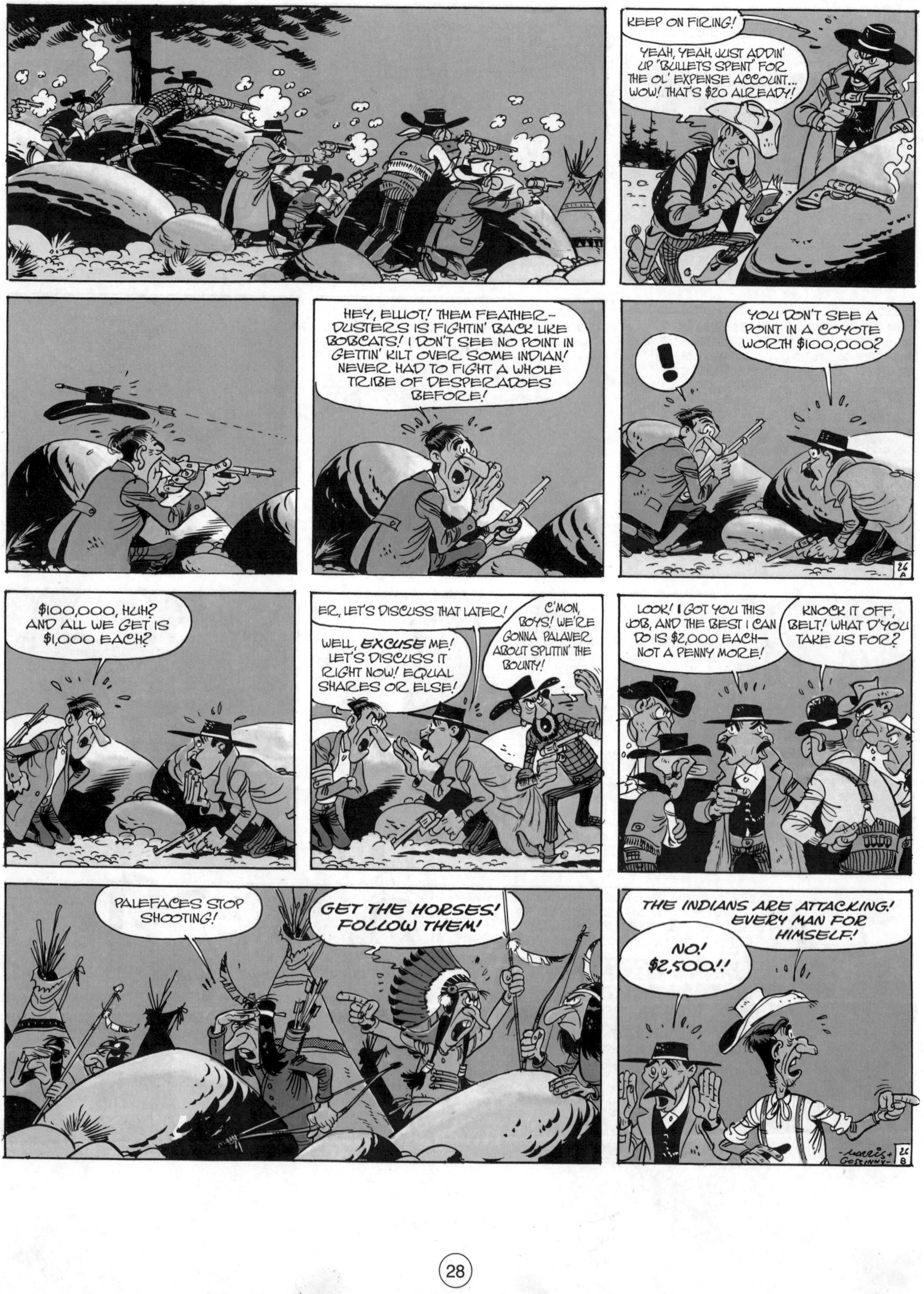
KEEP ON FIRING!
YEAH, YEAH. JUST ADDIN' UP "BULLETS SPENT" FOR THE OL' EXPENSE ACCOUNT... WOW! THAT'S $20 ALREADY!
HEY, ELLIOT! THEM FEATHER-DUSTERS IS FIGHTIN' BACK LIKE BOBCATS! I DON'T SEE NO POINT IN GETTIN' KILT OVER SOME INDIAN! NEVER HAD TO FIGHT A WHOLE TRIBE OF DESPERADOES BEFORE!
!
YOU DON'T SEE A POINT IN A COYOTE WORTH $100,000?
$100,000, HUH? AND ALL WE GET IS $1,000 EACH?
ER, LET'S DISCUSS THAT LATER!
WELL, EXCUSE ME! LET'S DISCUSS IT RIGHT NOW! EQUAL SHARES OR ELSE!
C'MON, BOYS! WE'RE GONNA PALAVER ABOUT SPLITTIN' THE BOUNTY!
LOOK! I GOT YOU THIS JOB, AND THE BEST I CAN DO IS $2,000 EACH— NOT A PENNY MORE!
KNOCK IT OFF, BELT! WHAT D'YOU TAKE US FOR?
PALEFACES STOP SHOOTING!
GET THE HORSES! FOLLOW THEM!
THE INDIANS ARE ATTACKING! EVERY MAN FOR HIMSELF!
NO! $2,500!!

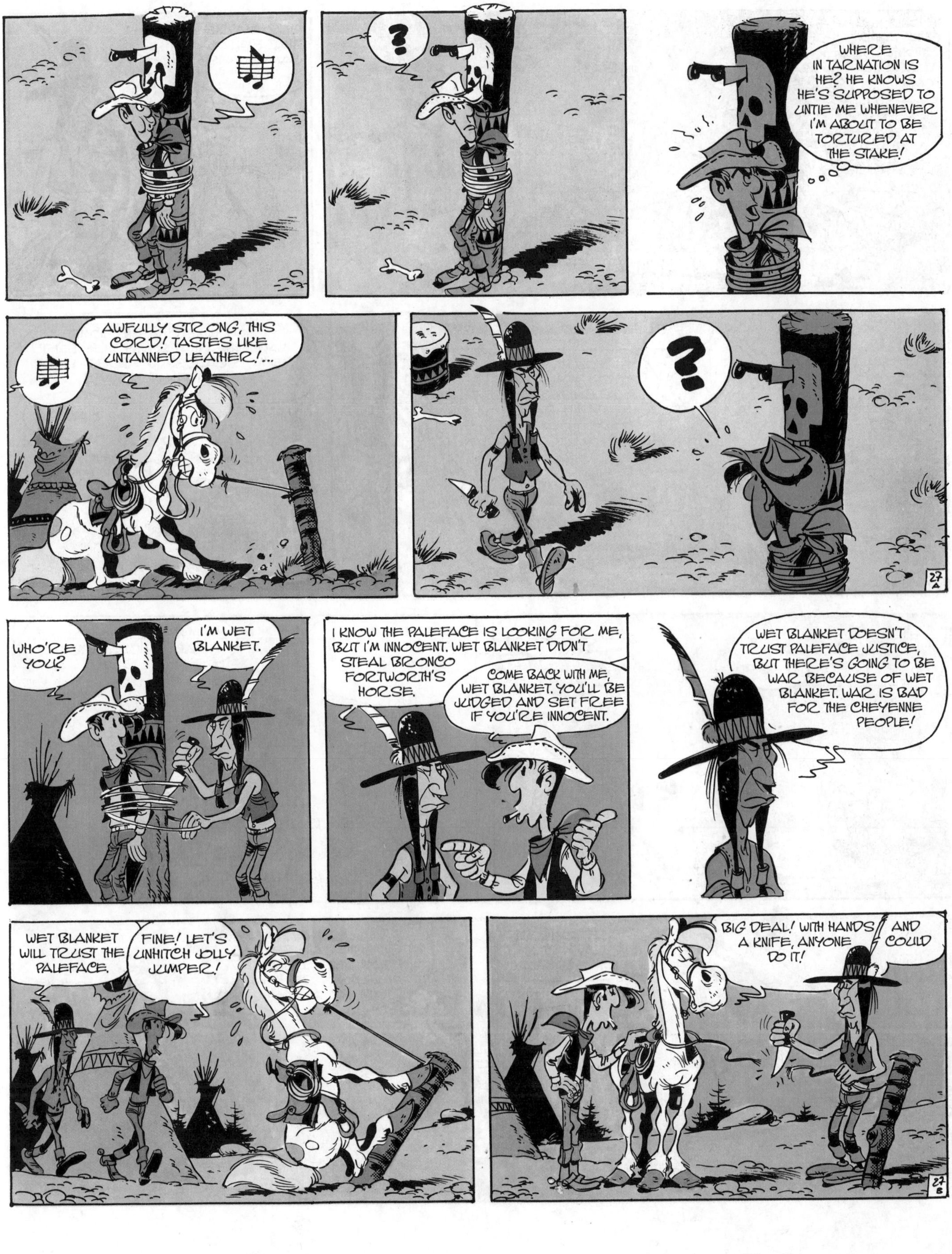
WHERE IN TARNATION IS HE? HE KNOWS HE'S SUPPOSED TO UNTIE ME WHENEVER I'M ABOUT TO BE TORTURED AT THE STAKE!
AWFULLY STRONG, THIS CORD! TASTES LIKE UNTANNED LEATHER!...
WHO'RE YOU?
I'M WET BLANKET.
I KNOW THE PALEFACE IS LOOKING FOR ME, BUT I'M INNOCENT. WET BLANKET DIDN'T STEAL BRONCO FORTWORTH'S HORSE.
COME BACK WITH ME, WET BLANKET. YOU'LL BE JUDGED AND SET FREE IF YOU'RE INNOCENT.
WET BLANKET DOESN'T TRUST PALEFACE JUSTICE, BUT THERE'S GOING TO BE WAR BECAUSE OF WET BLANKET. WAR IS BAD FOR THE CHEYENNE PEOPLE!
WET BLANKET WILL TRUST THE PALEFACE.
FINE! LET'S UNHITCH JOLLY JUMPER!
BIG DEAL! WITH HANDS AND A KNIFE, ANYONE COULD DO IT!

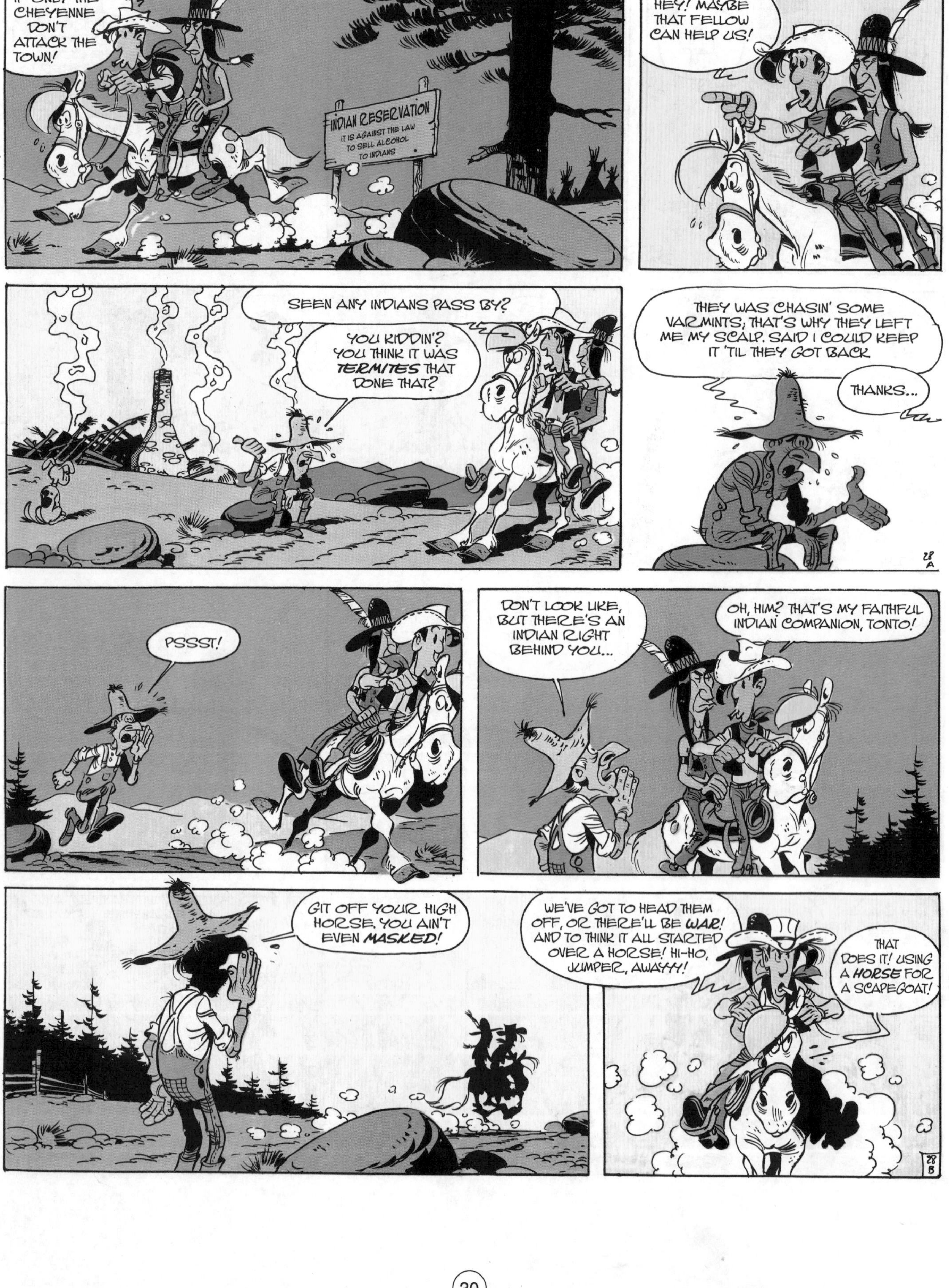
IF ONLY THE CHEYENNE DON'T ATTACK THE TOWN!
INDIAN RESERVATION
IT IS AGAINST THE LAW TO SELL ALCOHOL TO INDIANS
HEY! MAYBE THAT FELLOW CAN HELP US!
SEEN ANY INDIANS PASS BY?
YOU KIDDIN'? YOU THINK IT WAS TERMITES THAT DONE THAT?
THEY WAS CHASIN' SOME VARMINTS; THAT'S WHY THEY LEFT ME MY SCALP. SAID I COULD KEEP IT 'TIL THEY GOT BACK
THANKS...
PSSST!
DON'T LOOK LIKE, BUT THERE'S AN INDIAN RIGHT BEHIND YOU...
OH, HIM? THAT'S MY FAITHFUL INDIAN COMPANION, TONTO!
GIT OFF YOUR HIGH HORSE. YOU AIN'T EVEN MASKED!
WE'VE GOT TO HEAD THEM OFF, OR THERE'LL BE WAR! AND TO THINK IT ALL STARTED OVER A HORSE! HI-HO, JUMPER, AWAYYY!
THAT DOES IT! USING A HORSE FOR A SCAPEGOAT!

THE CHEYENNE! THEY LEFT THE RESERVATION! THEY'RE HEADED RIGHT FOR TOWN!

$3,075!!

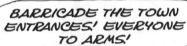

BARRICADE THE TOWN ENTRANCES! EVERYONE TO ARMS!

IN EVERY WESTERN TOWN, THE HARDY PIONEERS WERE WELL PREPARED FOR INDIAN ATTACKS...

THE LADIES' AUXILIARIES LEAP INTO ACTION.

FOOD IS RATIONED IN CASE OF SIEGE...

2 1/2 APPLES PER FAMILY

GROCERIES, FEED & PRODUCT

GO GET THE CAVALRY!

THEY'RE MIGHTY FAR AWAY. HOPE YOU FOLKS CAN HOLD OUT...

THEY'RE HIDING IN TOWN! WE'LL ATTACK!

WE'RE GOING BACK TO THE BIG TIPI!

AND HOW! WHERE THE WOMEN DO THE JIGGLE-JIGGLE DANCE!

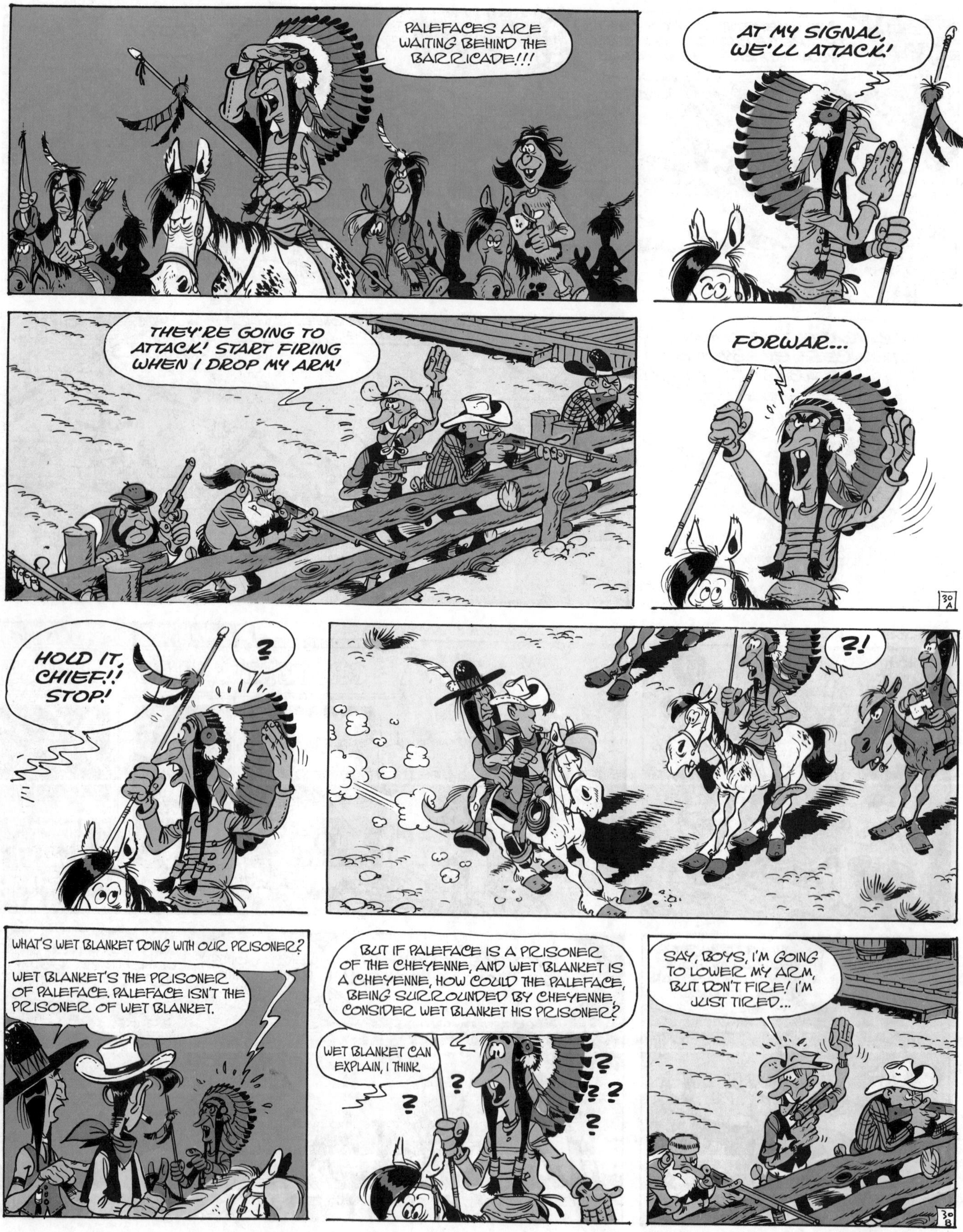
PALEFACES ARE WAITING BEHIND THE BARRICADE!!!
AT MY SIGNAL, WE'LL ATTACK!
THEY'RE GOING TO ATTACK! START FIRING WHEN I DROP MY ARM!
FORWAR...
30 A
HOLD IT, CHIEF!! STOP!
?
?!
WHAT'S WET BLANKET DOING WITH OUR PRISONER?
WET BLANKET'S THE PRISONER OF PALEFACE. PALEFACE ISN'T THE PRISONER OF WET BLANKET.
BUT IF PALEFACE IS A PRISONER OF THE CHEYENNE, AND WET BLANKET IS A CHEYENNE, HOW COULD THE PALEFACE, BEING SURROUNDED BY CHEYENNE, CONSIDER WET BLANKET HIS PRISONER?
WET BLANKET CAN EXPLAIN, I THINK.
? ? ? ? ? ?
SAY, BOYS, I'M GOING TO LOWER MY ARM, BUT DON'T FIRE! I'M JUST TIRED...
30 B

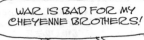

WAR IS BAD FOR MY CHEYENNE BROTHERS!

NOT AT ALL!

WET BLANKET IS A WET BLANKET!

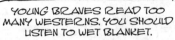

YOUNG BRAVES READ TOO MANY WESTERNS. YOU SHOULD LISTEN TO WET BLANKET.

BUFFALO CHIPS! WAR STIMULATES THE ECONOMY!

SMALL FLY AND HARD HEAD, STOP FLAPPING YOUR TONGUES! YOUNG BRAVES TALK TOO MUCH! NOW THE CHIEF WILL PUT A WET BLANKET ON!

LET'S HOLD A POW WOW IN THE BIG TIPI, OVER A CUP OF...

MY CHEYENNE BROTHERS, GO BACK TO THE RESERVATION. ONLY WET BLANKET IS INVOLVED HERE! IF HE'S INNOCENT, THE PALEFACE JUSTICE WILL LET HIM GO FREE...

PALEFACE-WITHOUT-A-THUNDER-STICK PROMISES A FAIR TRIAL FOR WET BLANKET, SO THE CHEYENNE MUST TRUST THE PALEFACE!

THE INDIANS ARE LEAVING! THERE'S NOT GONNA BE A WAR!

GOOD TIMES ARE BACK! TAKE ALL YOU WANT!

GROCERIES

FIRE SALE ON APPLES

PRE-WAR APPLES, EH? THEY LOOK KINDA WORMY...

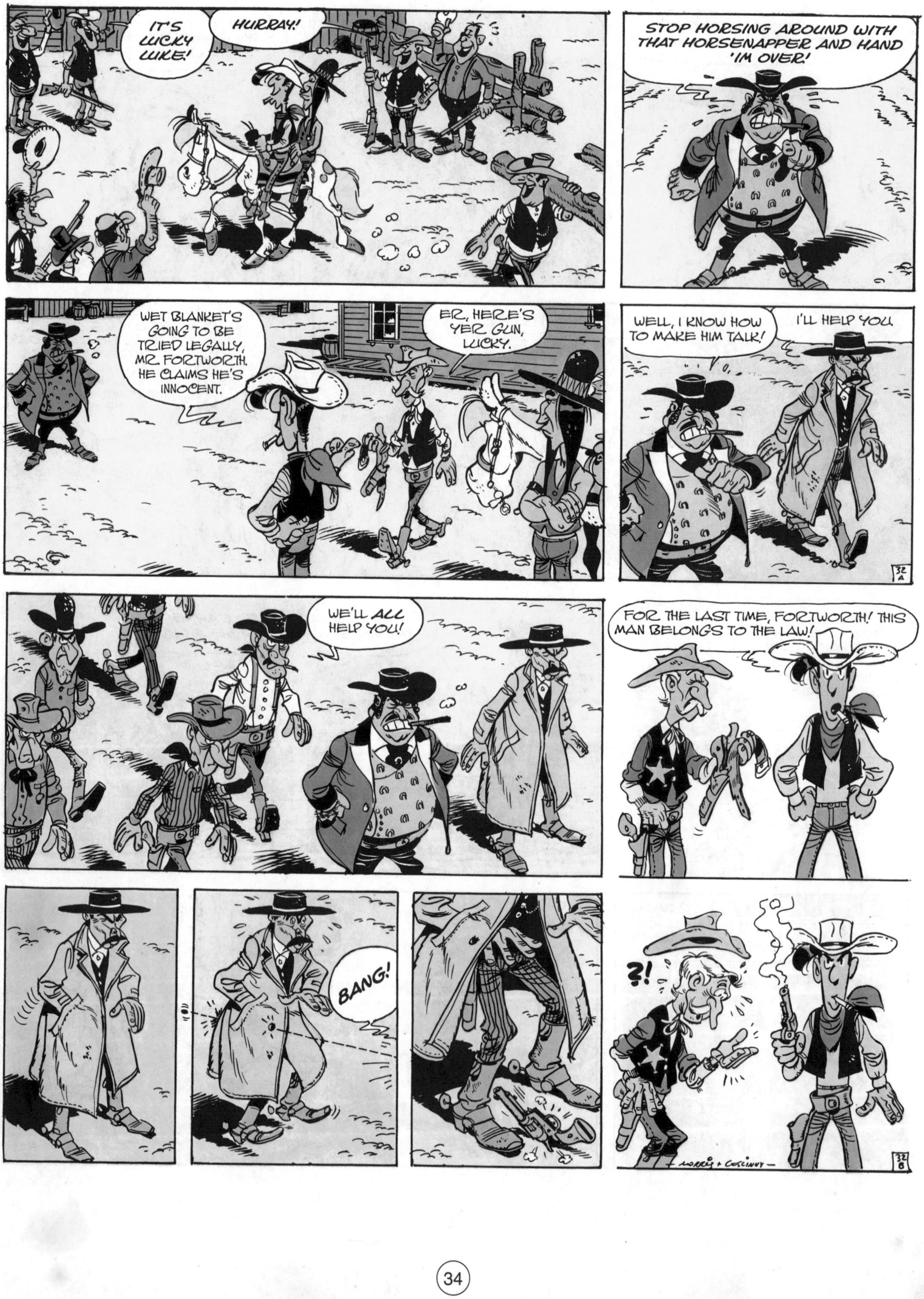
IT'S LUCKY LUKE!
HURRAY!
STOP HORSING AROUND WITH THAT HORSENAPPER AND HAND 'IM OVER!
WET BLANKET'S GOING TO BE TRIED LEGALLY, MR. FORTWORTH. HE CLAIMS HE'S INNOCENT.
ER, HERE'S YER GUN, LUCKY.
WELL, I KNOW HOW TO MAKE HIM TALK!
I'LL HELP YOU.
WE'LL ALL HELP YOU!
FOR THE LAST TIME, FORTWORTH! THIS MAN BELONGS TO THE LAW!
BANG!
?!

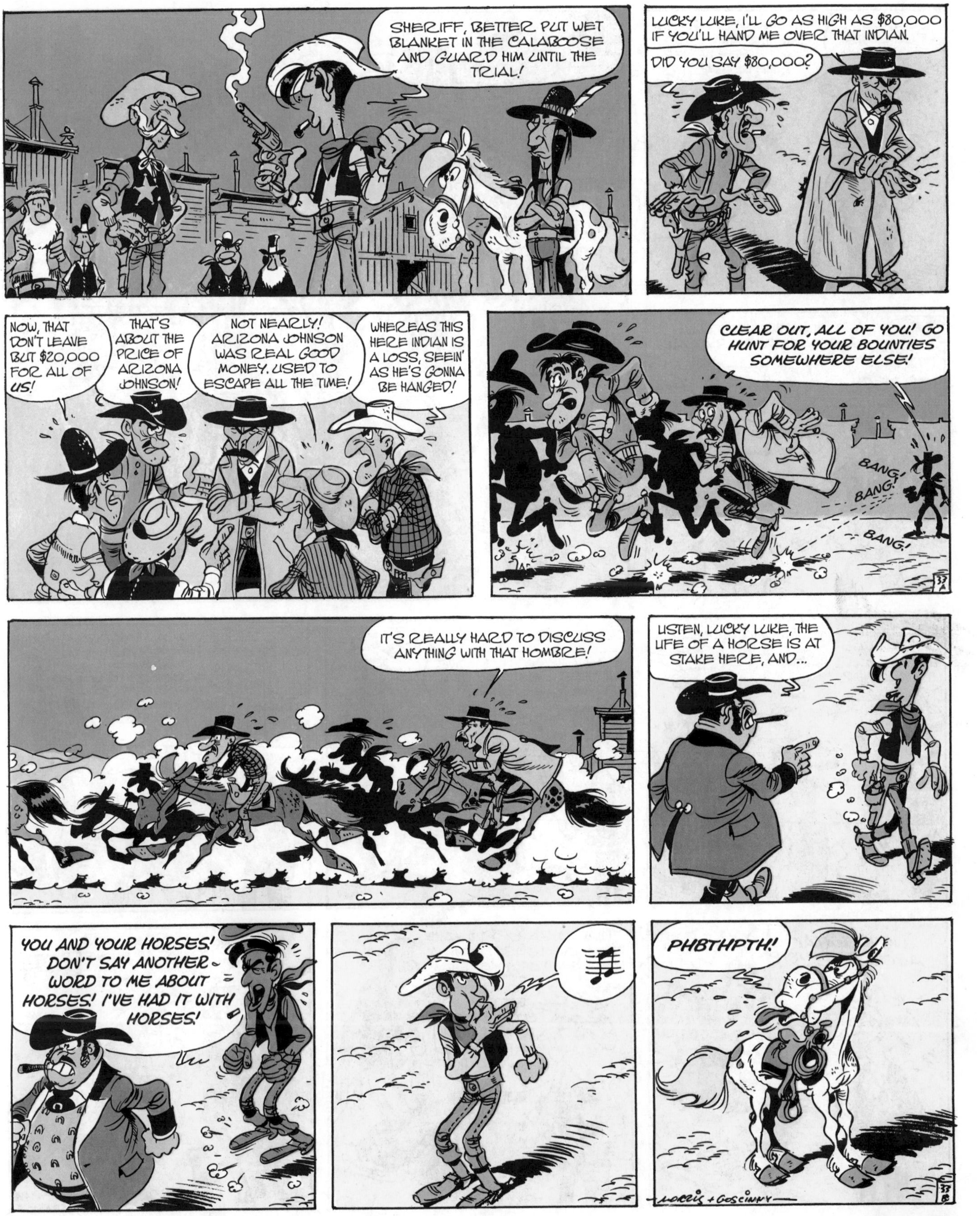
SHERIFF, BETTER PUT WET BLANKET IN THE CALABOOSE AND GUARD HIM UNTIL THE TRIAL!
LUCKY LUKE, I'LL GO AS HIGH AS $80,000 IF YOU'LL HAND ME OVER THAT INDIAN.
DID YOU SAY $80,000?
NOW, THAT DON'T LEAVE BUT $20,000 FOR ALL OF US!
THAT'S ABOUT THE PRICE OF ARIZONA JOHNSON!
NOT NEARLY! ARIZONA JOHNSON WAS REAL GOOD MONEY. USED TO ESCAPE ALL THE TIME!
WHEREAS THIS HERE INDIAN IS A LOSS, SEEIN' AS HE'S GONNA BE HANGED!
CLEAR OUT, ALL OF YOU! GO HUNT FOR YOUR BOUNTIES SOMEWHERE ELSE!
BANG!
BANG!
BANG!
IT'S REALLY HARD TO DISCUSS ANYTHING WITH THAT HOMBRE!
LISTEN, LUCKY LUKE, THE LIFE OF A HORSE IS AT STAKE HERE, AND...
YOU AND YOUR HORSES! DON'T SAY ANOTHER WORD TO ME ABOUT HORSES! I'VE HAD IT WITH HORSES!
PHBTHPTH!
MORRIS + GOSCINNY

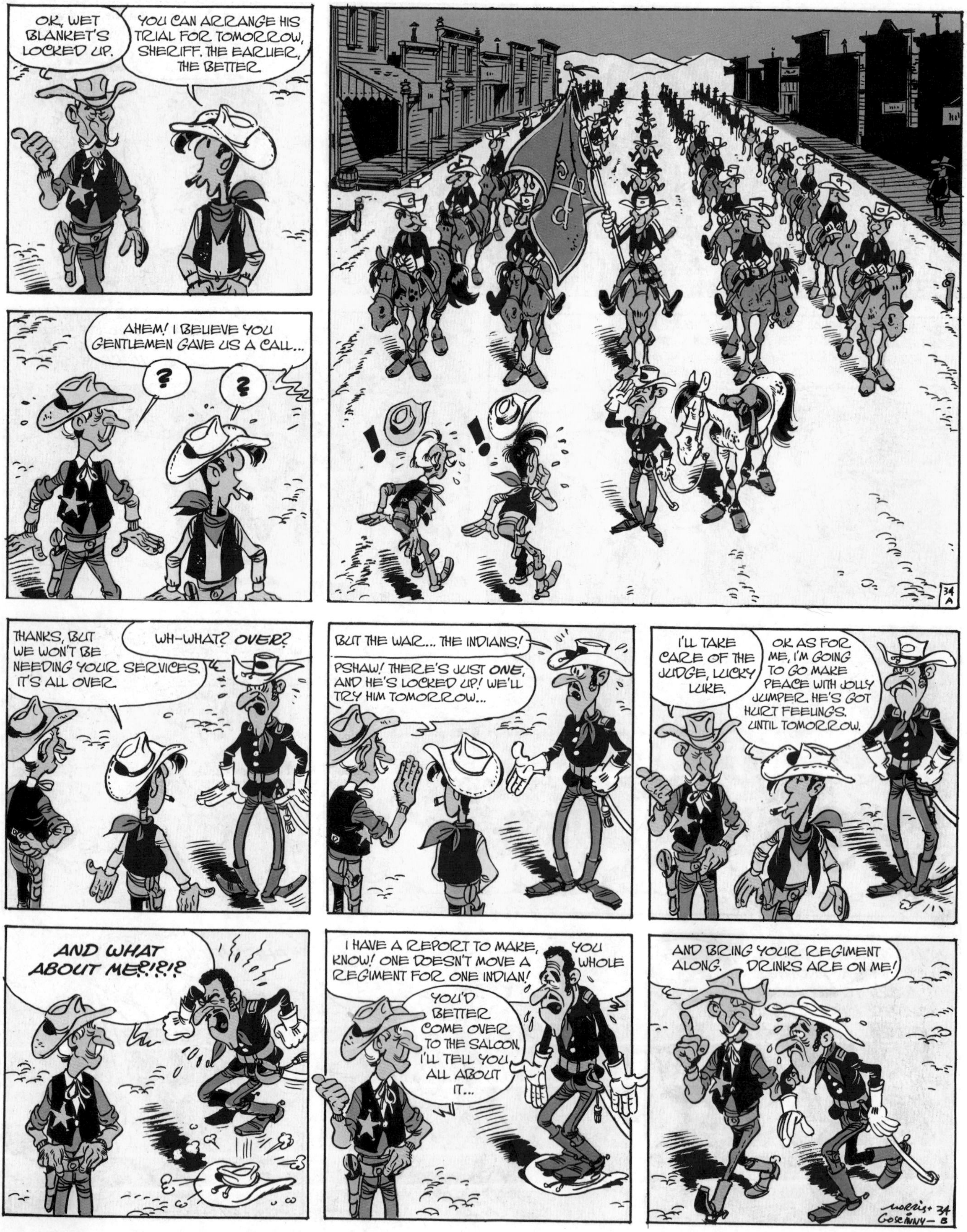
O.K., WET BLANKET'S LOCKED UP.
YOU CAN ARRANGE HIS TRIAL FOR TOMORROW, SHERIFF. THE EARLIER, THE BETTER.
AHEM! I BELIEVE YOU GENTLEMEN GAVE US A CALL...
?
?
!
!
34 A
THANKS, BUT WE WON'T BE NEEDING YOUR SERVICES. IT'S ALL OVER.
WH-WHAT? OVER?
BUT THE WAR... THE INDIANS!
PSHAW! THERE'S JUST ONE, AND HE'S LOCKED UP! WE'LL TRY HIM TOMORROW...
I'LL TAKE CARE OF THE JUDGE, LUCKY LUKE.
O.K. AS FOR ME, I'M GOING TO GO MAKE PEACE WITH JOLLY JUMPER. HE'S GOT HURT FEELINGS. UNTIL TOMORROW.
AND WHAT ABOUT ME?!?!?
I HAVE A REPORT TO MAKE, YOU KNOW! ONE DOESN'T MOVE A WHOLE REGIMENT FOR ONE INDIAN!
YOU'D BETTER COME OVER TO THE SALOON. I'LL TELL YOU ALL ABOUT IT...
AND BRING YOUR REGIMENT ALONG. DRINKS ARE ON ME!
morris + Goscinny 34 B

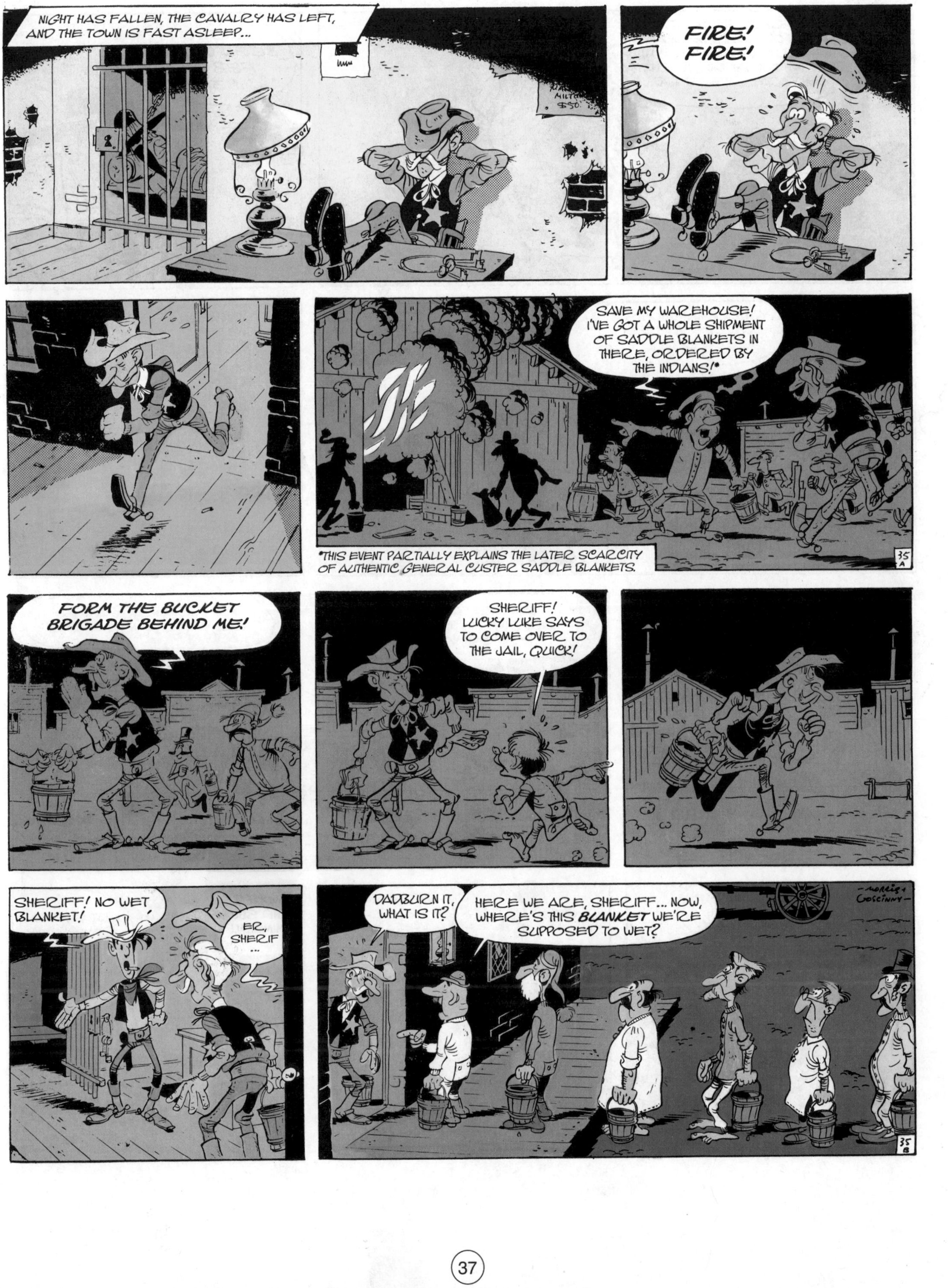
NIGHT HAS FALLEN, THE CAVALRY HAS LEFT, AND THE TOWN IS FAST ASLEEP...
FIRE! FIRE!
SAVE MY WAREHOUSE! I'VE GOT A WHOLE SHIPMENT OF SADDLE BLANKETS IN THERE, ORDERED BY THE INDIANS!*
*THIS EVENT PARTIALLY EXPLAINS THE LATER SCARCITY OF AUTHENTIC GENERAL CUSTER SADDLE BLANKETS.
FORM THE BUCKET BRIGADE BEHIND ME!
SHERIFF! LUCKY LUKE SAYS TO COME OVER TO THE JAIL, QUICK!
SHERIFF! NO WET BLANKET!
ER, SHERIF ...
DADBURN IT, WHAT IS IT?
HERE WE ARE, SHERIFF... NOW, WHERE'S THIS BLANKET WE'RE SUPPOSED TO WET?

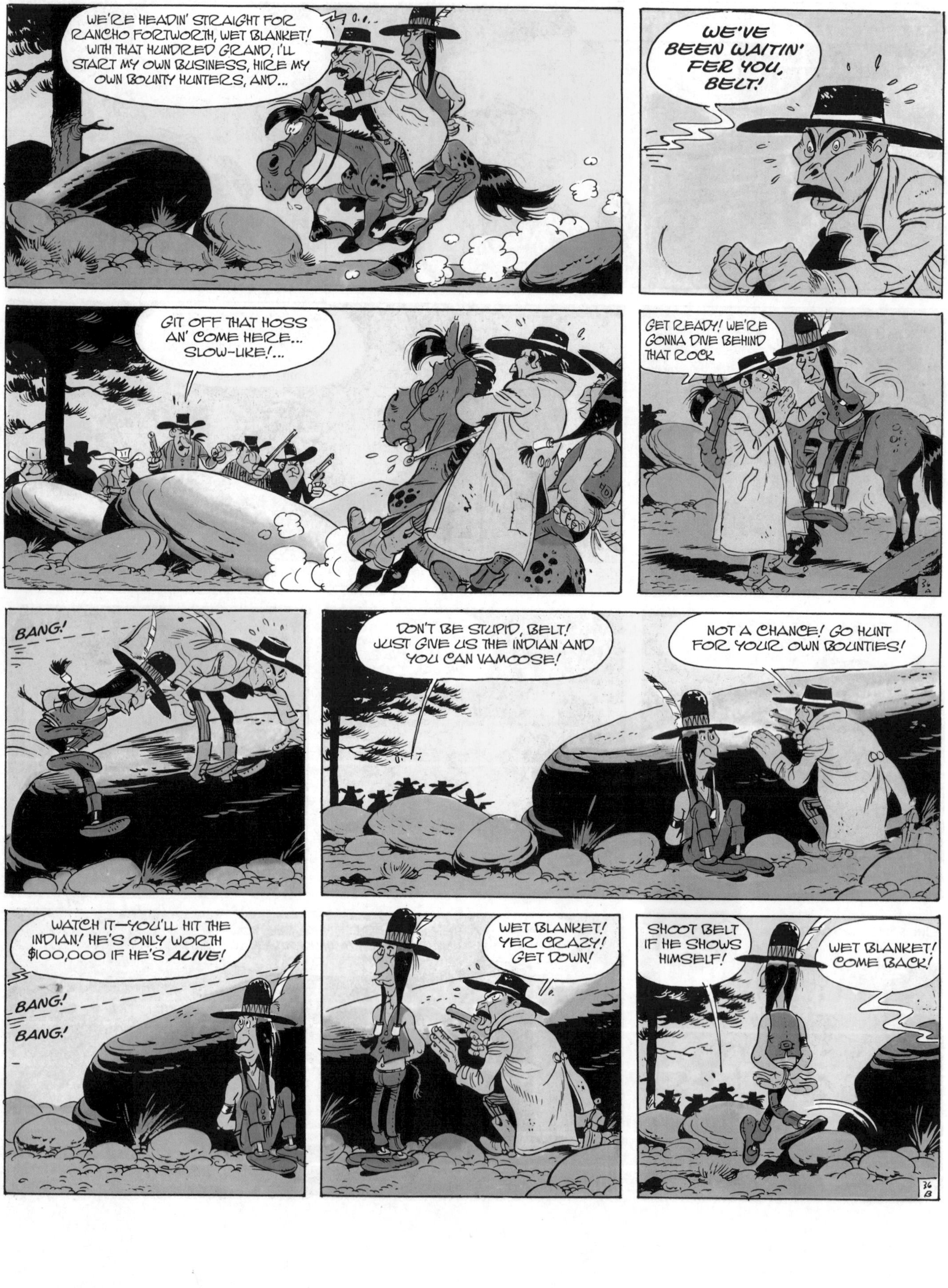
WE'RE HEADIN' STRAIGHT FOR RANCHO FORTWORTH, WET BLANKET! WITH THAT HUNDRED GRAND, I'LL START MY OWN BUSINESS, HIRE MY OWN BOUNTY HUNTERS, AND...
WE'VE BEEN WAITIN' FER YOU, BELT!
GIT OFF THAT HOSS AN' COME HERE... SLOW-LIKE!...
GET READY! WE'RE GONNA DIVE BEHIND THAT ROCK
BANG!
DON'T BE STUPID, BELT! JUST GIVE US THE INDIAN AND YOU CAN VAMOOSE!
NOT A CHANCE! GO HUNT FOR YOUR OWN BOUNTIES!
WATCH IT—YOU'LL HIT THE INDIAN! HE'S ONLY WORTH $100,000 IF HE'S ALIVE!
BANG!
BANG!
WET BLANKET! YER CRAZY! GET DOWN!
SHOOT BELT IF HE SHOWS HIMSELF!
WET BLANKET! COME BACK!

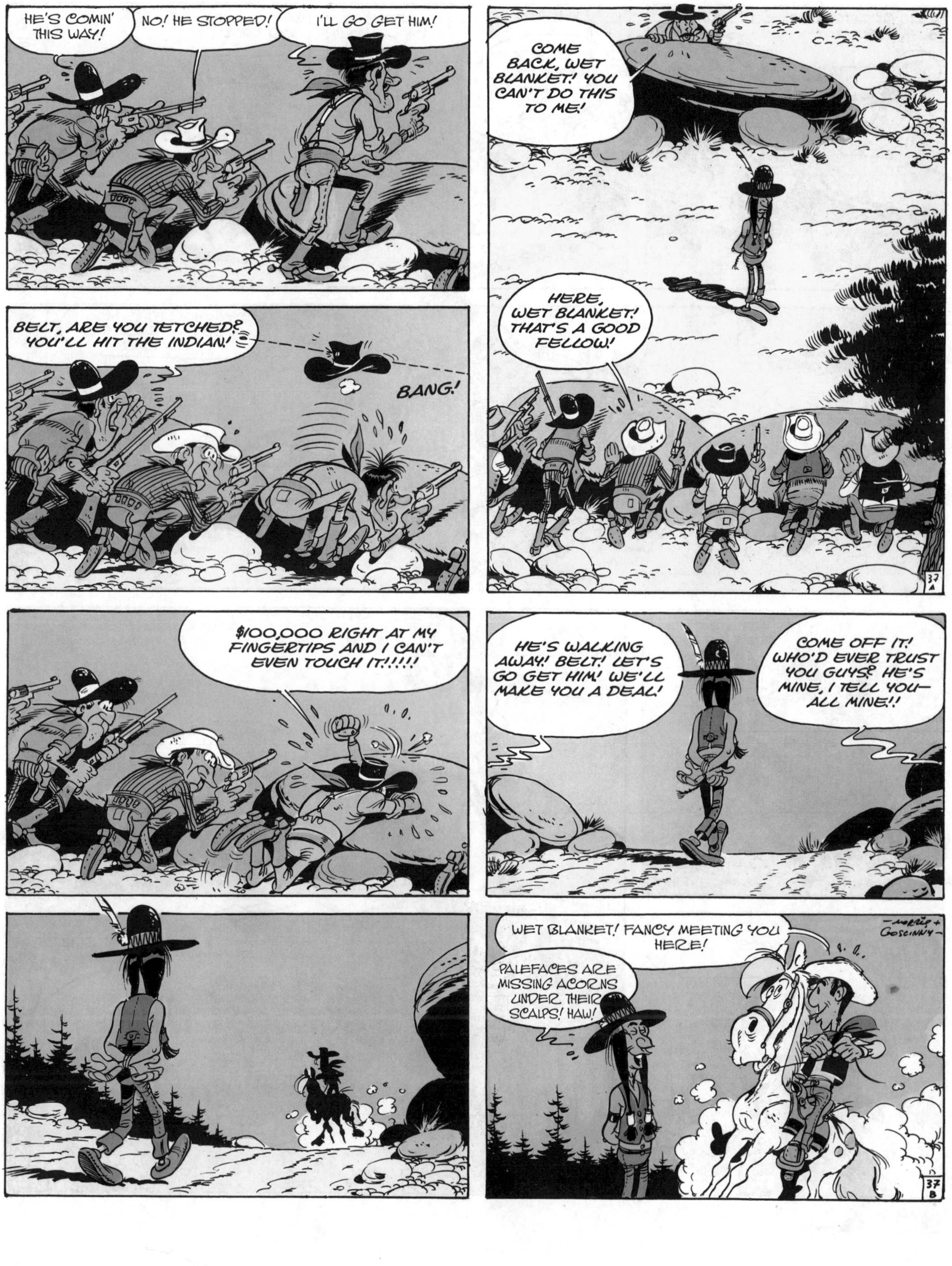

HE'S COMIN' THIS WAY!
NO! HE STOPPED!
I'LL GO GET HIM!
COME BACK, WET BLANKET! YOU CAN'T DO THIS TO ME!
BELT, ARE YOU TETCHED? YOU'LL HIT THE INDIAN!
BANG!
HERE, WET BLANKET! THAT'S A GOOD FELLOW!
37 A
$100,000 RIGHT AT MY FINGERTIPS AND I CAN'T EVEN TOUCH IT!!!!!
HE'S WALKING AWAY! BELT! LET'S GO GET HIM! WE'LL MAKE YOU A DEAL!
COME OFF IT! WHO'D EVER TRUST YOU GUYS? HE'S MINE, I TELL YOU— ALL MINE!!
WET BLANKET! FANCY MEETING YOU HERE!
PALEFACES ARE MISSING ACORNS UNDER THEIR SCALPS! HAW!
—MORRIS + GOSCINNY—
37 B

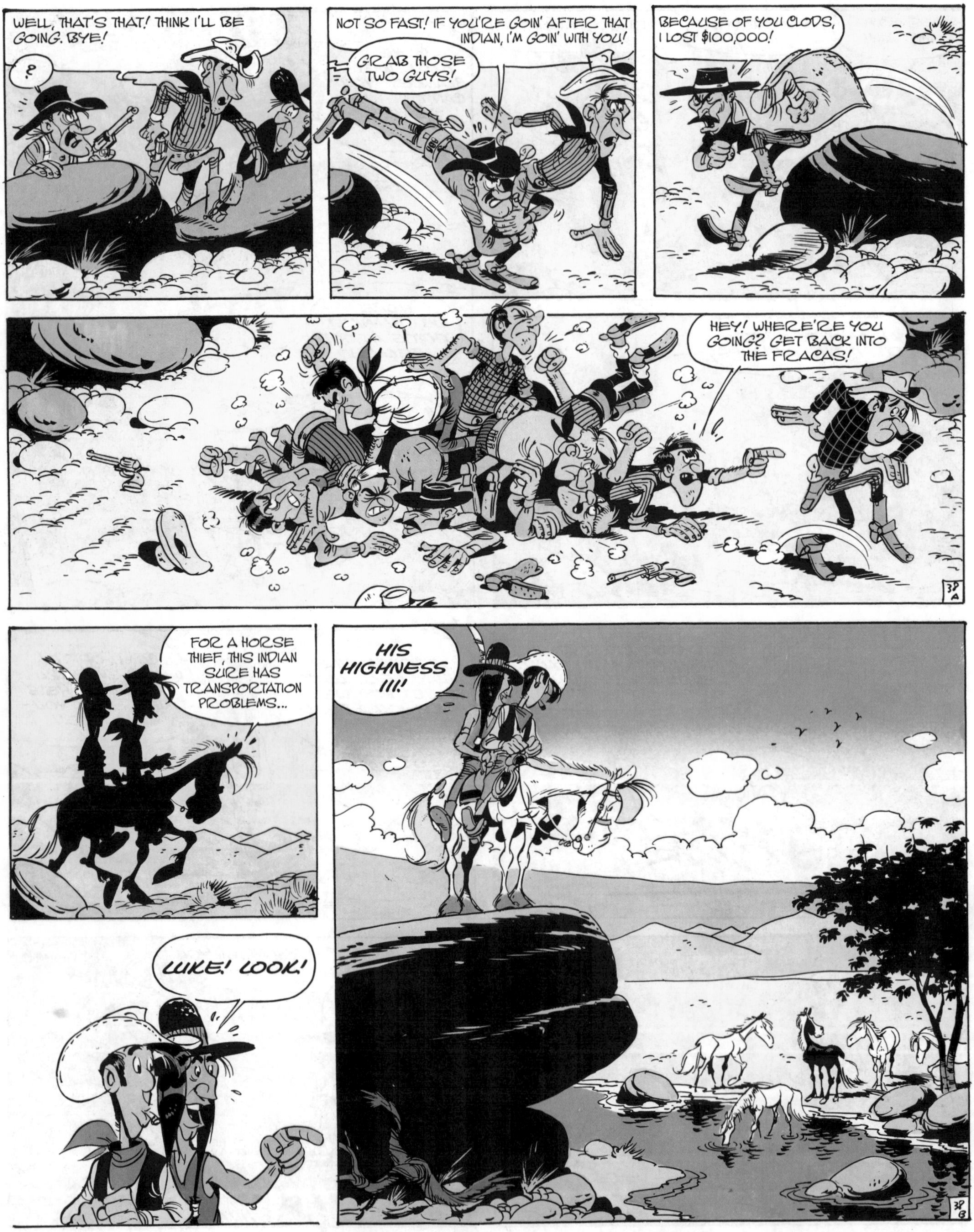
WELL, THAT'S THAT! THINK I'LL BE GOING. BYE!
?
NOT SO FAST! IF YOU'RE GOIN' AFTER THAT INDIAN, I'M GOIN' WITH YOU!
GRAB THOSE TWO GUYS!
BECAUSE OF YOU CLODS, I LOST $100,000!
HEY! WHERE'RE YOU GOING? GET BACK INTO THE FRACAS!
FOR A HORSE THIEF, THIS INDIAN SURE HAS TRANSPORTATION PROBLEMS...
LUKE! LOOK!
HIS HIGHNESS III!

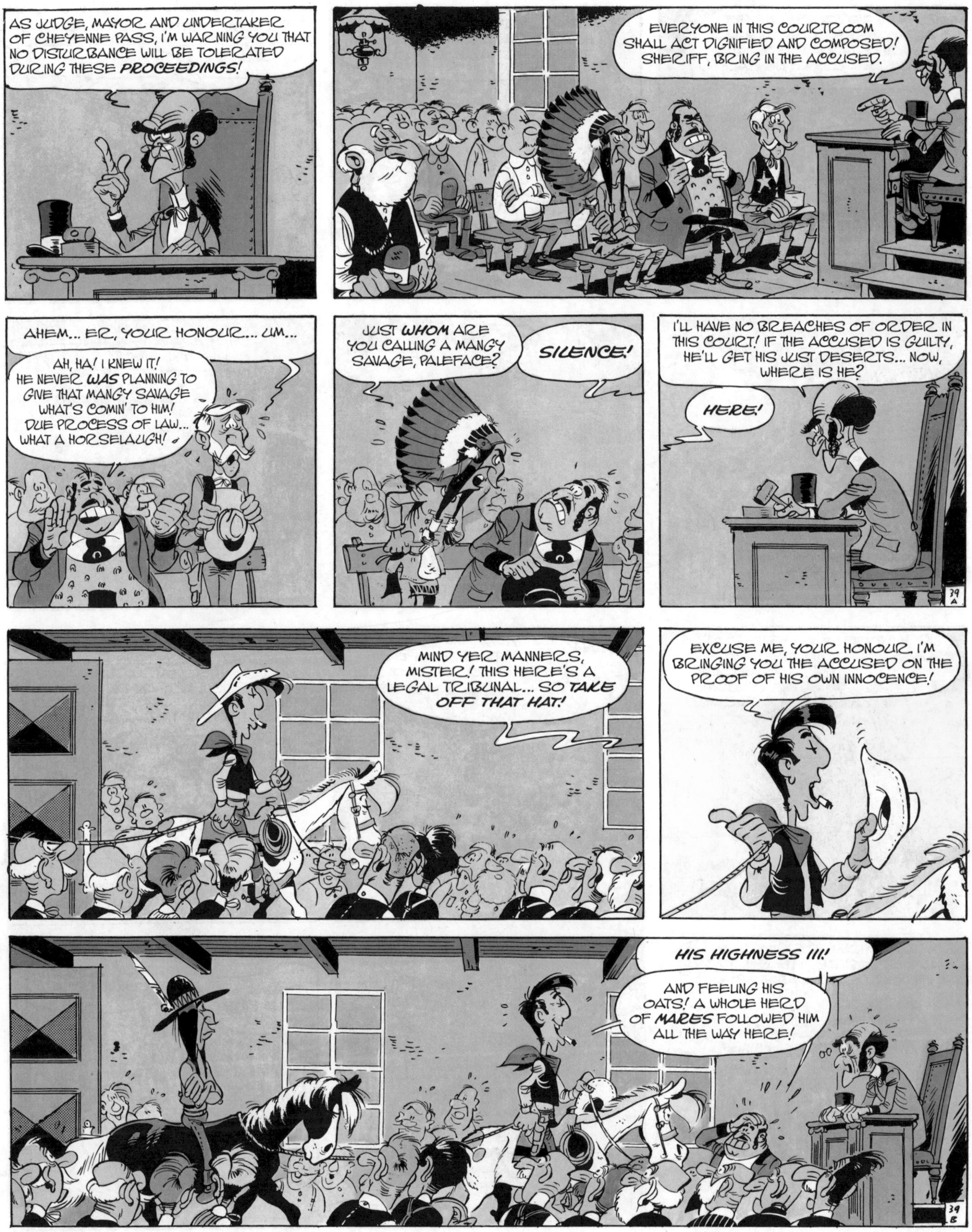

AS JUDGE, MAYOR AND UNDERTAKER OF CHEYENNE PASS, I'M WARNING YOU THAT NO DISTURBANCE WILL BE TOLERATED DURING THESE PROCEEDINGS!
EVERYONE IN THIS COURTROOM SHALL ACT DIGNIFIED AND COMPOSED! SHERIFF, BRING IN THE ACCUSED.
AHEM... ER, YOUR HONOUR... UM...
AH, HA! I KNEW IT! HE NEVER WAS PLANNING TO GIVE THAT MANGY SAVAGE WHAT'S COMIN' TO HIM! DUE PROCESS OF LAW... WHAT A HORSELAUGH!
JUST WHOM ARE YOU CALLING A MANGY SAVAGE, PALEFACE?
SILENCE!
I'LL HAVE NO BREACHES OF ORDER IN THIS COURT! IF THE ACCUSED IS GUILTY, HE'LL GET HIS JUST DESERTS... NOW, WHERE IS HE?
HERE!
MIND YER MANNERS, MISTER! THIS HERE'S A LEGAL TRIBUNAL... SO TAKE OFF THAT HAT!
EXCUSE ME, YOUR HONOUR. I'M BRINGING YOU THE ACCUSED ON THE PROOF OF HIS OWN INNOCENCE!
HIS HIGHNESS III!
AND FEELING HIS OATS! A WHOLE HERD OF MARES FOLLOWED HIM ALL THE WAY HERE!

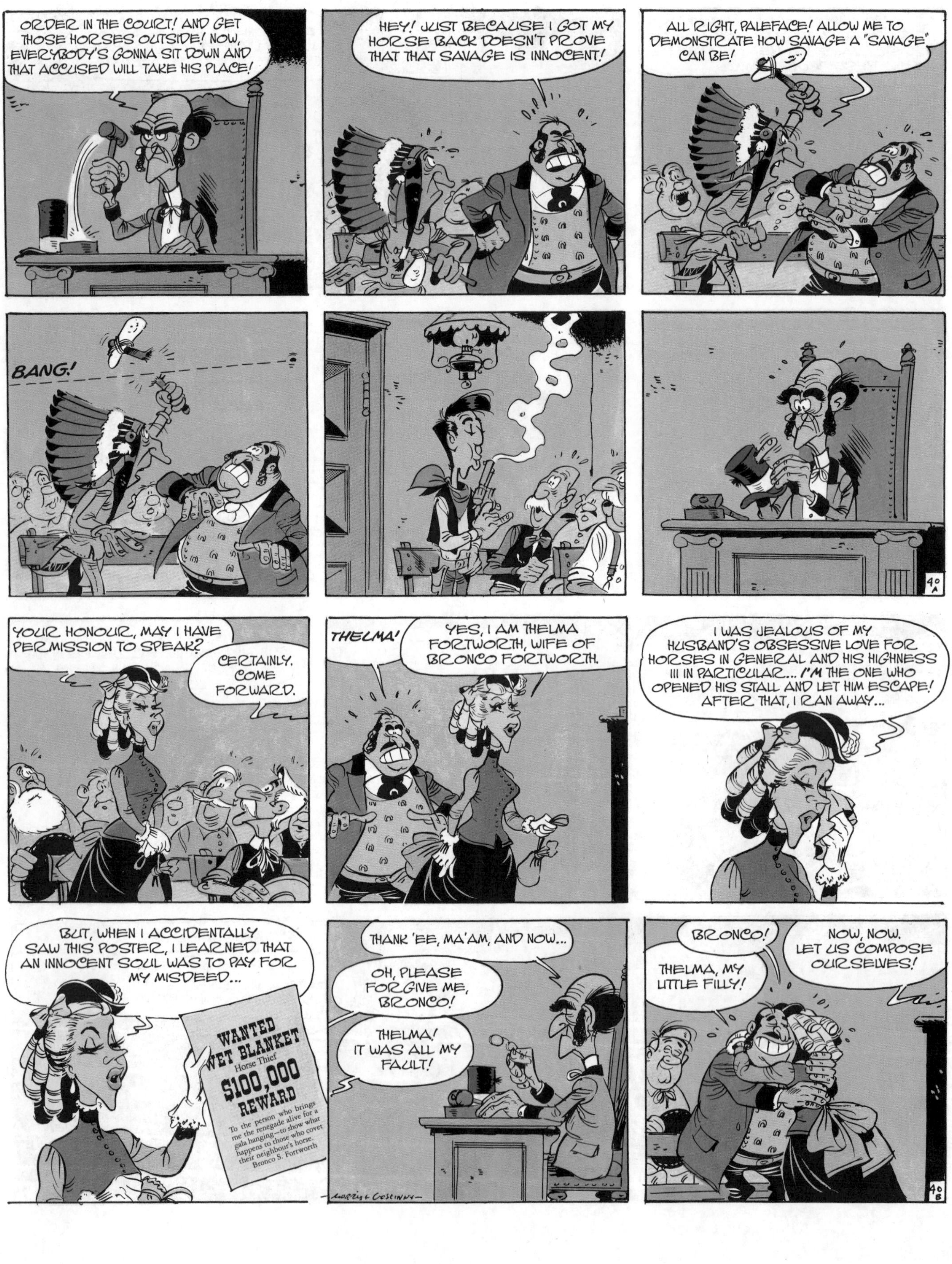
ORDER IN THE COURT! AND GET THOSE HORSES OUTSIDE! NOW, EVERYBODY'S GONNA SIT DOWN AND THAT ACCUSED WILL TAKE HIS PLACE!
HEY! JUST BECAUSE I GOT MY HORSE BACK DOESN'T PROVE THAT THAT SAVAGE IS INNOCENT!
ALL RIGHT, PALEFACE! ALLOW ME TO DEMONSTRATE HOW SAVAGE A "SAVAGE" CAN BE!
BANG!
YOUR HONOUR, MAY I HAVE PERMISSION TO SPEAK?
CERTAINLY. COME FORWARD.
THELMA!
YES, I AM THELMA FORTWORTH, WIFE OF BRONCO FORTWORTH.
I WAS JEALOUS OF MY HUSBAND'S OBSESSIVE LOVE FOR HORSES IN GENERAL AND HIS HIGHNESS III IN PARTICULAR... I'M THE ONE WHO OPENED HIS STALL AND LET HIM ESCAPE! AFTER THAT, I RAN AWAY...
BUT, WHEN I ACCIDENTALLY SAW THIS POSTER, I LEARNED THAT AN INNOCENT SOUL WAS TO PAY FOR MY MISDEED...
WANTED
WET BLANKET
Horse Thief
$100,000
REWARD
To the person who brings me the renegade alive for a gala hanging—to show what happens to those who covet their neighbour's horse.
Bronco S. Forrworth
THANK 'EE, MA'AM, AND NOW...
OH, PLEASE FORGIVE ME, BRONCO!
THELMA! IT WAS ALL MY FAULT!
BRONCO!
THELMA, MY LITTLE FILLY!
NOW, NOW. LET US COMPOSE OURSELVES!

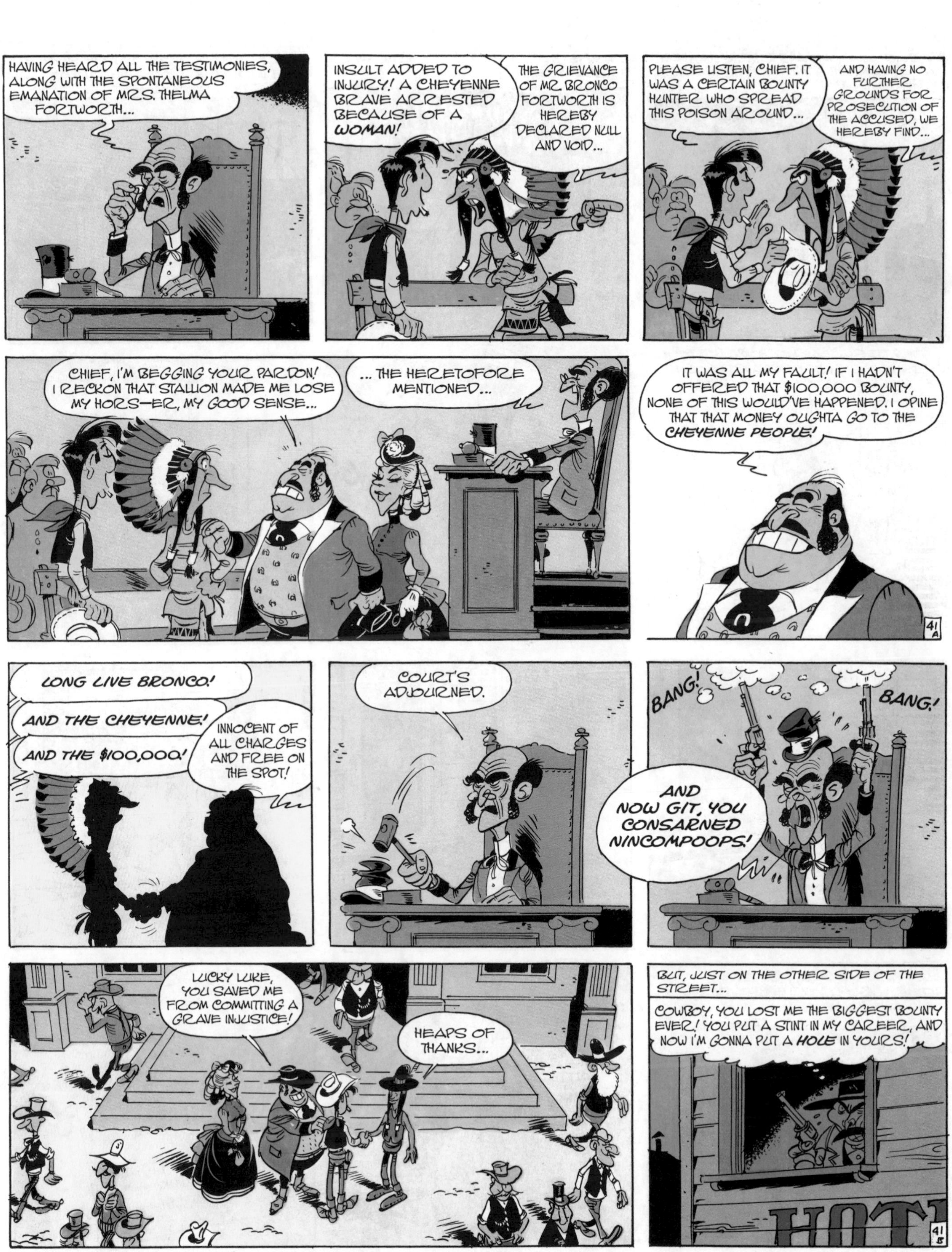
HAVING HEARD ALL THE TESTIMONIES, ALONG WITH THE SPONTANEOUS EMANATION OF MRS. THELMA FORTWORTH...
INSULT ADDED TO INJURY! A CHEYENNE BRAVE ARRESTED BECAUSE OF A WOMAN!
THE GRIEVANCE OF MR BRONCO FORTWORTH IS HEREBY DECLARED NULL AND VOID...
PLEASE LISTEN, CHIEF. IT WAS A CERTAIN BOUNTY HUNTER WHO SPREAD THIS POISON AROUND...
AND HAVING NO FURTHER GROUNDS FOR PROSECUTION OF THE ACCUSED, WE HEREBY FIND...
CHIEF, I'M BEGGING YOUR PARDON! I RECKON THAT STALLION MADE ME LOSE MY HORS—ER, MY GOOD SENSE...
... THE HERETOFORE MENTIONED...
IT WAS ALL MY FAULT! IF I HADN'T OFFERED THAT $100,000 BOUNTY, NONE OF THIS WOULD'VE HAPPENED. I OPINE THAT THAT MONEY OUGHTA GO TO THE CHEYENNE PEOPLE!
LONG LIVE BRONCO!
AND THE CHEYENNE!
AND THE $100,000!
INNOCENT OF ALL CHARGES AND FREE ON THE SPOT!
COURT'S ADJOURNED.
BANG!
BANG!
AND NOW GIT, YOU CONSARNED NINCOMPOOPS!
LUCKY LUKE, YOU SAVED ME FROM COMMITTING A GRAVE INJUSTICE!
HEAPS OF THANKS...
BUT, JUST ON THE OTHER SIDE OF THE STREET...
COWBOY, YOU LOST ME THE BIGGEST BOUNTY EVER! YOU PUT A STINT IN MY CAREER, AND NOW I'M GONNA PUT A HOLE IN YOURS!
HOT

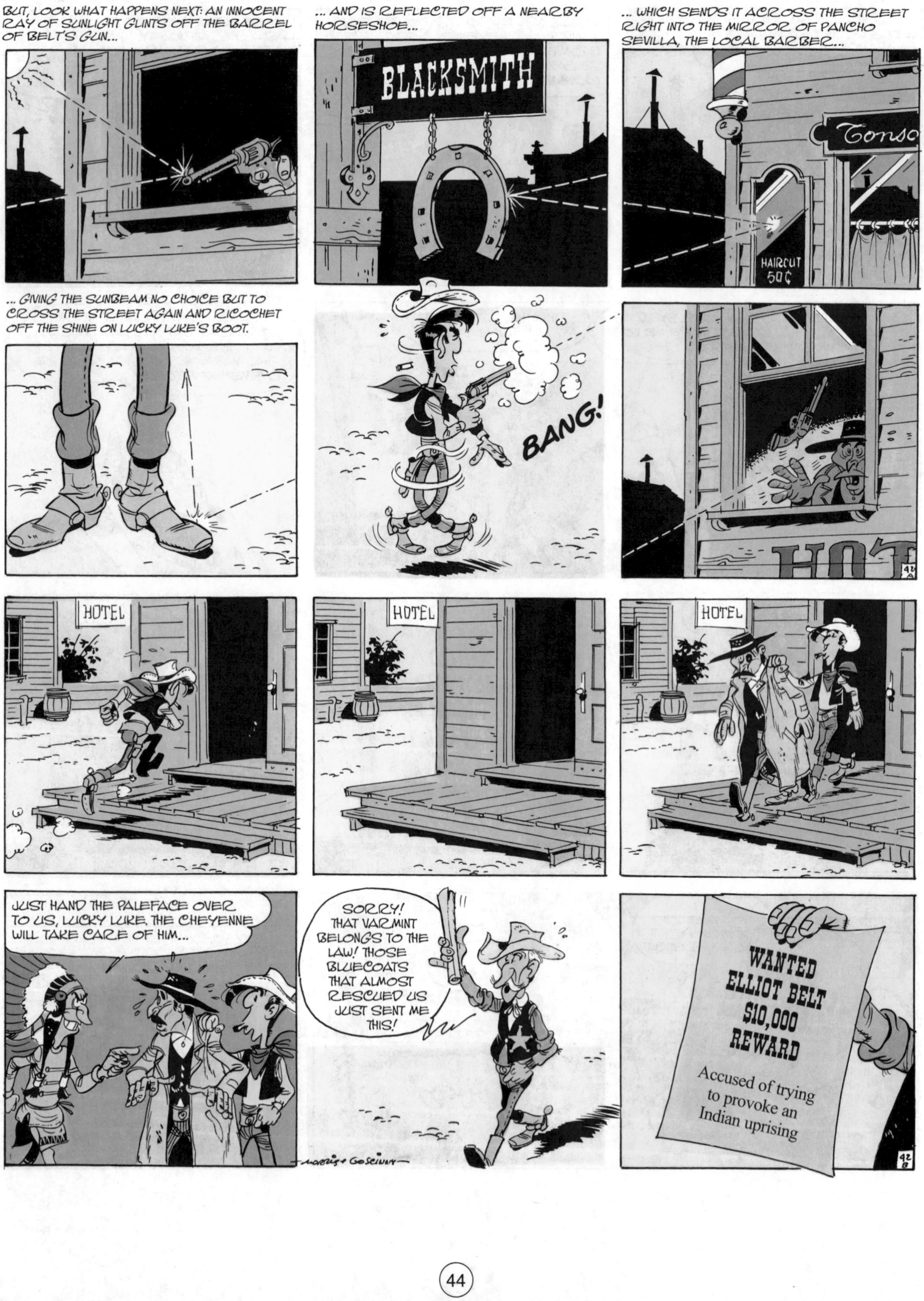
BUT, LOOK WHAT HAPPENS NEXT: AN INNOCENT RAY OF SUNLIGHT GLINTS OFF THE BARREL OF BELT'S GUN...
... AND IS REFLECTED OFF A NEARBY HORSESHOE...
BLACKSMITH
... WHICH SENDS IT ACROSS THE STREET RIGHT INTO THE MIRROR OF PANCHO SEVILLA, THE LOCAL BARBER...
HAIRCUT 50¢
... GIVING THE SUNBEAM NO CHOICE BUT TO CROSS THE STREET AGAIN AND RICOCHET OFF THE SHINE ON LUCKY LUKE'S BOOT.
BANG!
HOTEL
HOTEL
HOTEL
JUST HAND THE PALEFACE OVER TO US, LUCKY LUKE. THE CHEYENNE WILL TAKE CARE OF HIM...
SORRY! THAT VARMINT BELONGS TO THE LAW! THOSE BLUECOATS THAT ALMOST RESCUED US JUST SENT ME THIS!
WANTED ELLIOT BELT $10,000 REWARD
Accused of trying to provoke an Indian uprising

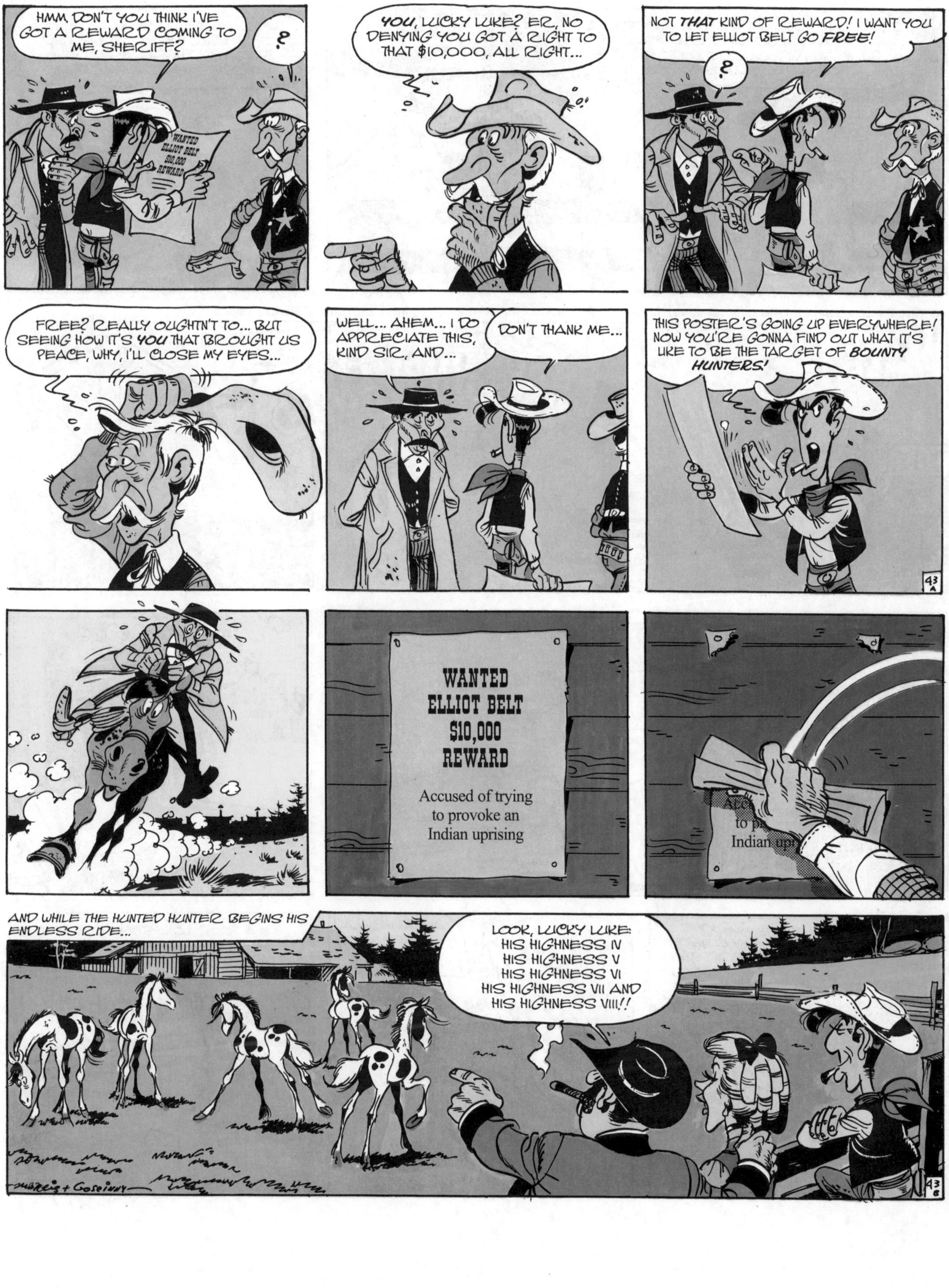
HMM, DON'T YOU THINK I'VE GOT A REWARD COMING TO ME, SHERIFF?
?
WANTED ELLIOT BELT $10,000 REWARD
YOU, LUCKY LUKE? ER, NO DENYING YOU GOT A RIGHT TO THAT $10,000, ALL RIGHT...
NOT THAT KIND OF REWARD! I WANT YOU TO LET ELLIOT BELT GO FREE!
?
FREE? REALLY OUGHTN'T TO... BUT SEEING HOW IT'S YOU THAT BROUGHT US PEACE, WHY, I'LL CLOSE MY EYES...
WELL... AHEM... I DO APPRECIATE THIS, KIND SIR, AND...
DON'T THANK ME...
THIS POSTER'S GOING UP EVERYWHERE! NOW YOU'RE GONNA FIND OUT WHAT IT'S LIKE TO BE THE TARGET OF BOUNTY HUNTERS!
WANTED
ELLIOT BELT
$10,000
REWARD
Accused of trying to provoke an Indian uprising
AND WHILE THE HUNTED HUNTER BEGINS HIS ENDLESS RIDE...
LOOK, LUCKY LUKE: HIS HIGHNESS IV HIS HIGHNESS V HIS HIGHNESS VI HIS HIGHNESS VII AND HIS HIGHNESS VIII!!

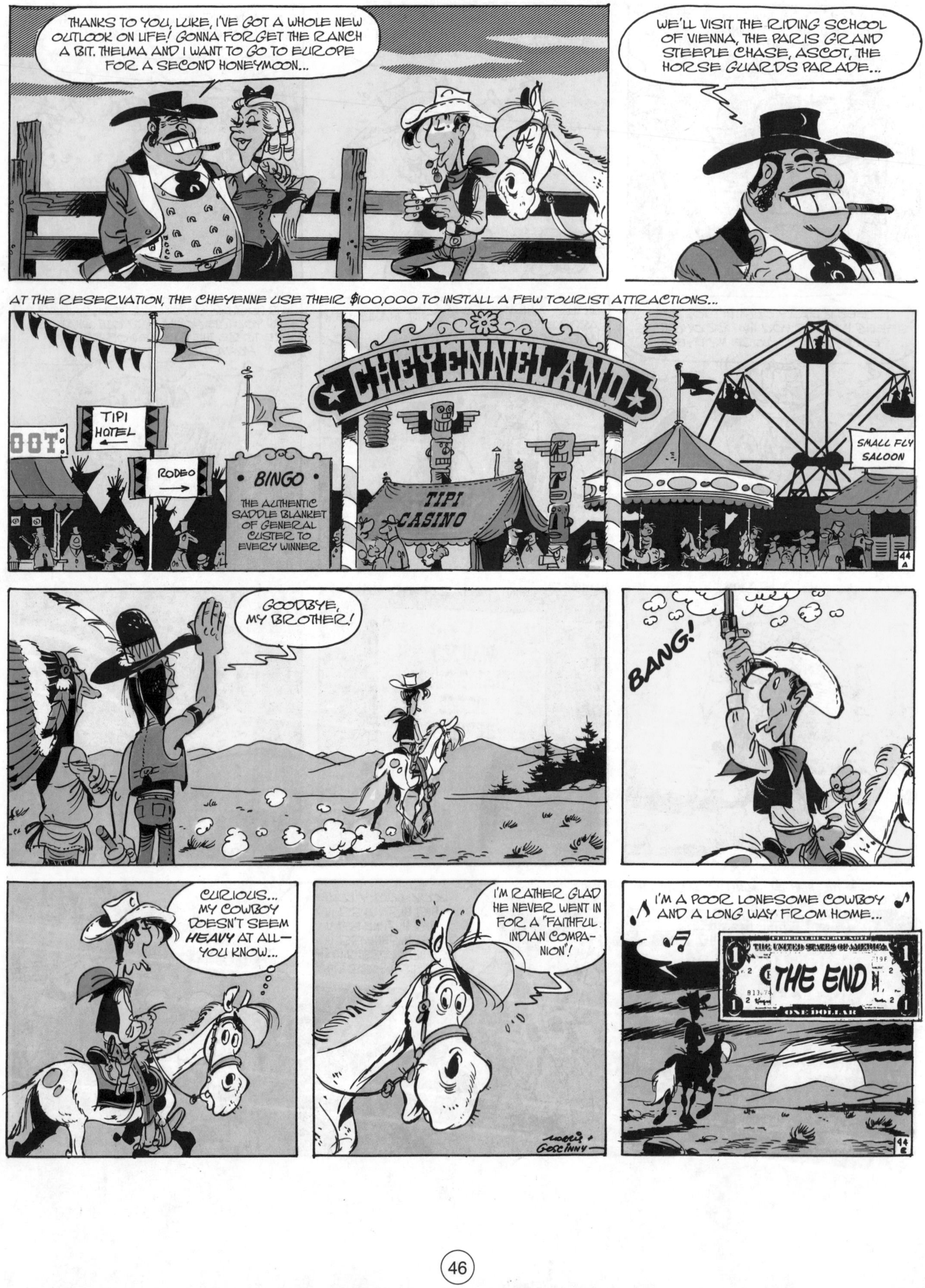
THANKS TO YOU, LUKE, I'VE GOT A WHOLE NEW OUTLOOK ON LIFE! GONNA FORGET THE RANCH A BIT. THELMA AND I WANT TO GO TO EUROPE FOR A SECOND HONEYMOON...
WE'LL VISIT THE RIDING SCHOOL OF VIENNA, THE PARIS GRAND STEEPLE CHASE, ASCOT, THE HORSE GUARDS PARADE...
AT THE RESERVATION, THE CHEYENNE USE THEIR $100,000 TO INSTALL A FEW TOURIST ATTRACTIONS...
CHEYENNELAND
TIPI HOTEL
RODEO
BINGO
THE AUTHENTIC SADDLE BLANKET OF GENERAL CUSTER TO EVERY WINNER
TIPI CASINO
SMALL FLY SALOON
GOODBYE, MY BROTHER!
BANG!
CURIOUS... MY COWBOY DOESN'T SEEM HEAVY AT ALL- YOU KNOW...
I'M RATHER GLAD HE NEVER WENT IN FOR A "FAITHFUL INDIAN COMPANION"!
I'M A POOR LONESOME COWBOY AND A LONG WAY FROM HOME...
THE END
ONE DOLLAR
MORRIS + GOSCINNY

CINEBOOK
The 9th Art Publisher

presents

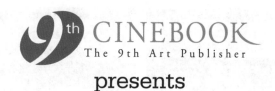

LUCKY LUKE

The man who shoots faster than his own shadow

A LUCKY LUKE ADVENTURE 1
BILLY the Kid
MORRIS & GOSCINNY
CINEBOOK

A LUCKY LUKE ADVENTURE 2
GHOST TOWN
MORRIS & GOSCINNY
CINEBOOK

A LUCKY LUKE ADVENTURE 3
DALTON CITY
MORRIS & GOSCINNY
CINEBOOK

A LUCKY LUKE ADVENTURE 4
JESSE JAMES
MORRIS & GOSCINNY
CINEBOOK

A LUCKY LUKE ADVENTURE 5
IN THE SHADOW OF THE DERRICKS
E. L. DRAKE OIL CO.
MORRIS & GOSCINNY
CINEBOOK

A LUCKY LUKE ADVENTURE 6
MA DALTON
MORRIS & GOSCINNY
WANTED
DALTON brothers
CINEBOOK

A LUCKY LUKE ADVENTURE 7
BARBED WIRE ON THE PRAIRIE
MORRIS & GOSCINNY
CINEBOOK

A LUCKY LUKE ADVENTURE 8
CALAMITY JANE
MORRIS & GOSCINNY
CINEBOOK

A LUCKY LUKE ADVENTURE 9
THE WAGON TRAIN
MORRIS & GOSCINNY
CINEBOOK

A LUCKY LUKE ADVENTURE 10
TORTILLAS FOR THE DALTONS
MORRIS & GOSCINNY
CINEBOOK

A LUCKY LUKE ADVENTURE 11
WESTERN CIRCUS
MORRIS & GOSCINNY
CINEBOOK

A LUCKY LUKE ADVENTURE 12
THE RIVALS OF PAINFUL GULCH
MORRIS & GOSCINNY
CINEBOOK

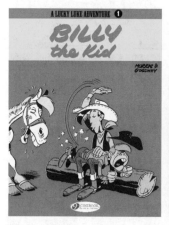

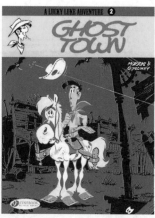

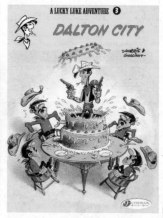

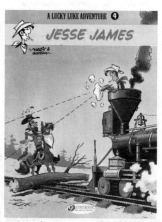

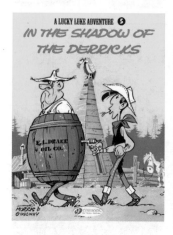

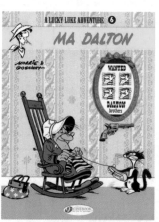

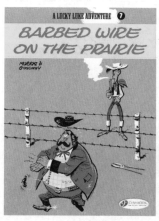

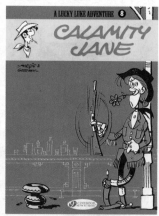

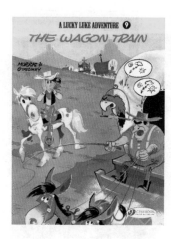

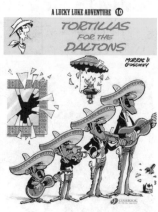

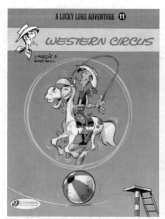

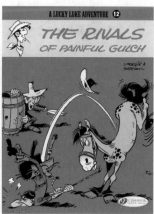

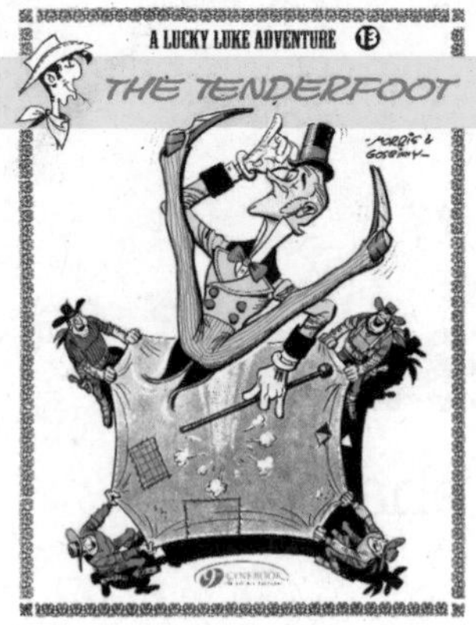
A LUCKY LUKE ADVENTURE 13
THE TENDERFOOT
MORRIS & GOSCINNY

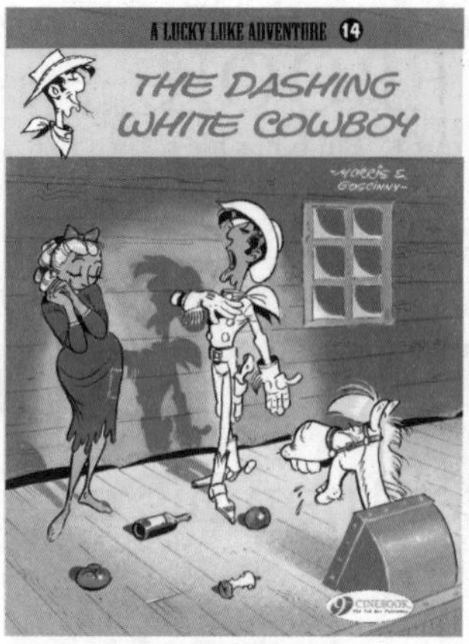
A LUCKY LUKE ADVENTURE 14
THE DASHING WHITE COWBOY
MORRIS & GOSCINNY

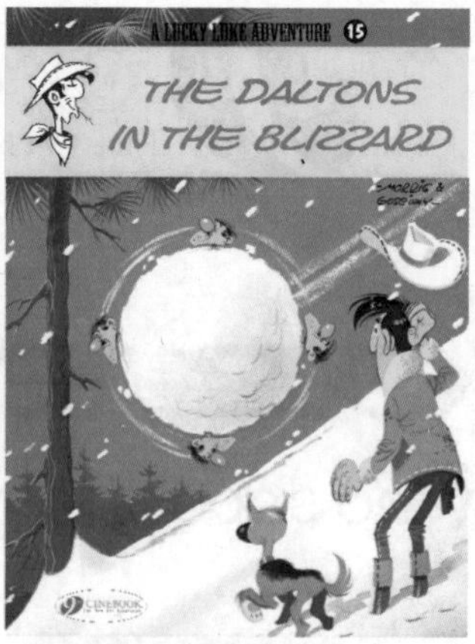
A LUCKY LUKE ADVENTURE 15
THE DALTONS IN THE BLIZZARD
MORRIS & GOSCINNY

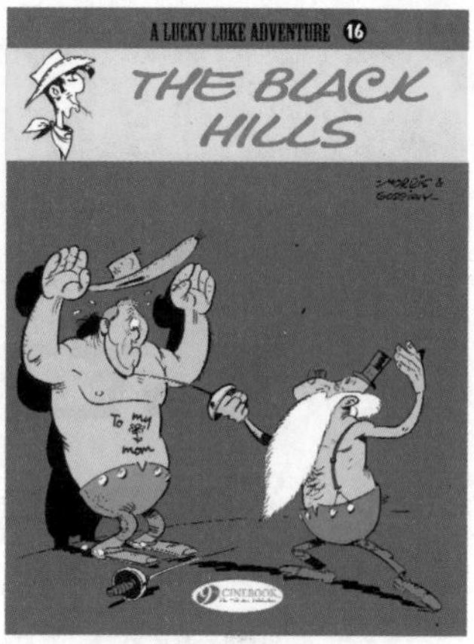
A LUCKY LUKE ADVENTURE 16
THE BLACK HILLS
MORRIS & GOSCINNY

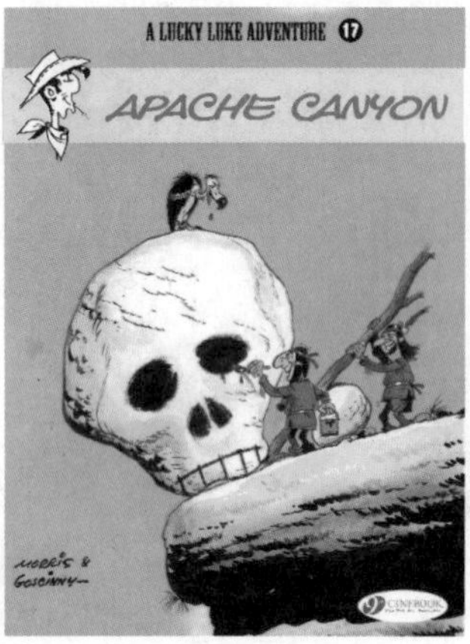
A LUCKY LUKE ADVENTURE 17
APACHE CANYON
MORRIS & GOSCINNY

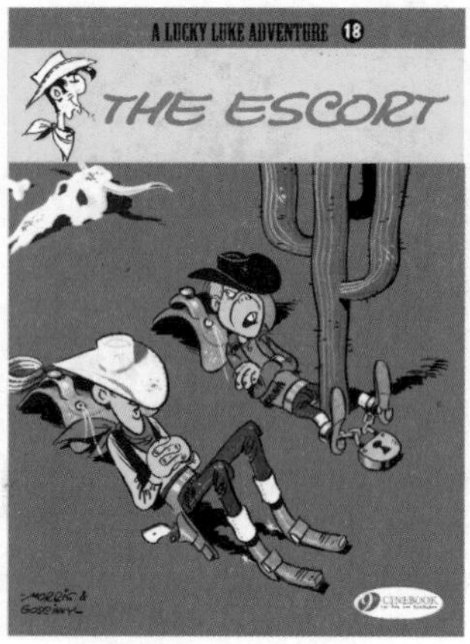
A LUCKY LUKE ADVENTURE 18
THE ESCORT
MORRIS & GOSCINNY

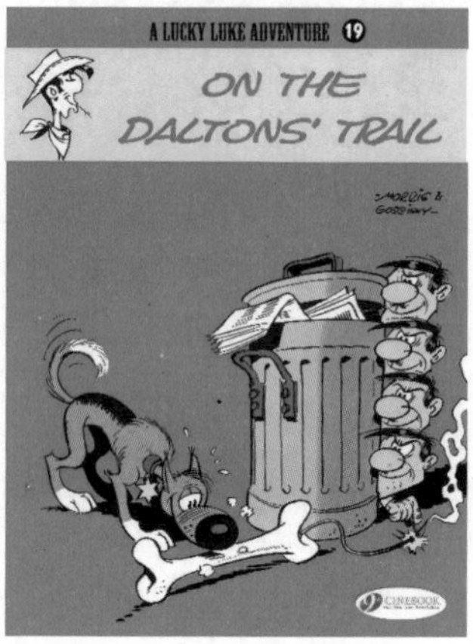
A LUCKY LUKE ADVENTURE 19
ON THE DALTONS' TRAIL
MORRIS & GOSCINNY

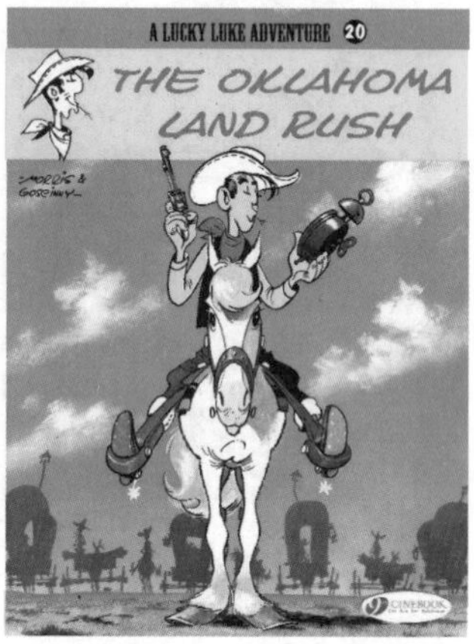
A LUCKY LUKE ADVENTURE 20
THE OKLAHOMA LAND RUSH
MORRIS & GOSCINNY

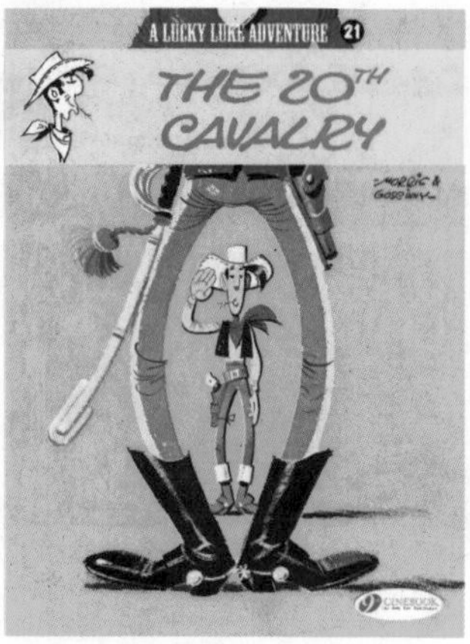
A LUCKY LUKE ADVENTURE 21
THE 20TH CAVALRY
MORRIS & GOSCINNY

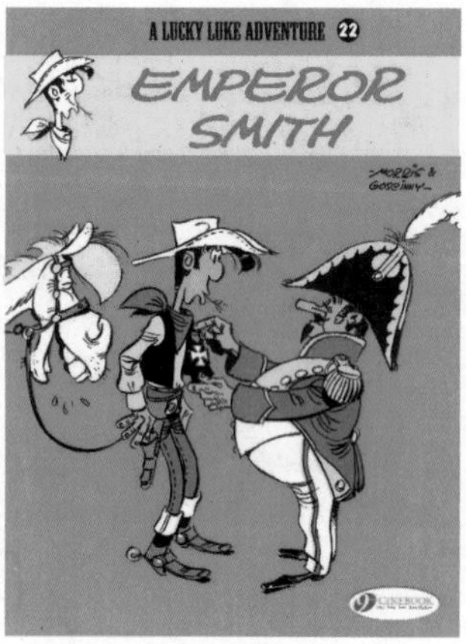
A LUCKY LUKE ADVENTURE 22
EMPEROR SMITH
MORRIS & GOSCINNY

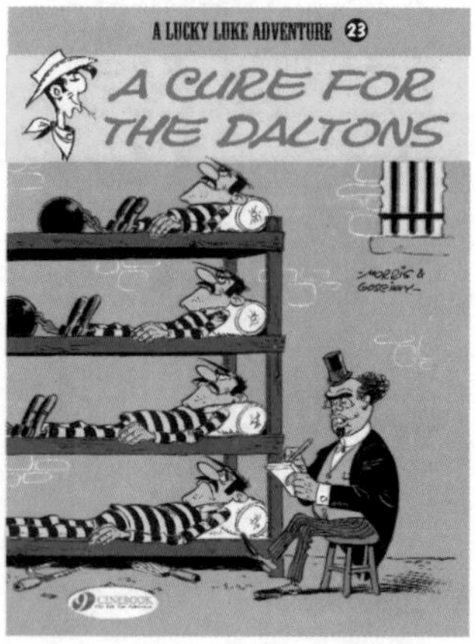
A LUCKY LUKE ADVENTURE 23
A CURE FOR THE DALTONS
MORRIS & GOSCINNY

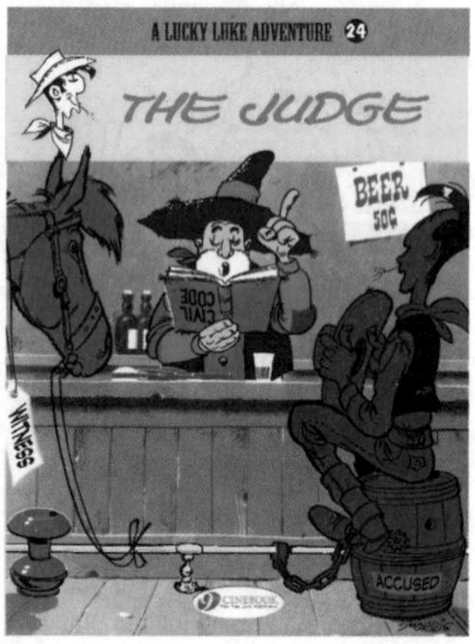
A LUCKY LUKE ADVENTURE 24
THE JUDGE
BEER 30¢
CODE CIVIL
WITNESS
ACCUSED

COMING SOON

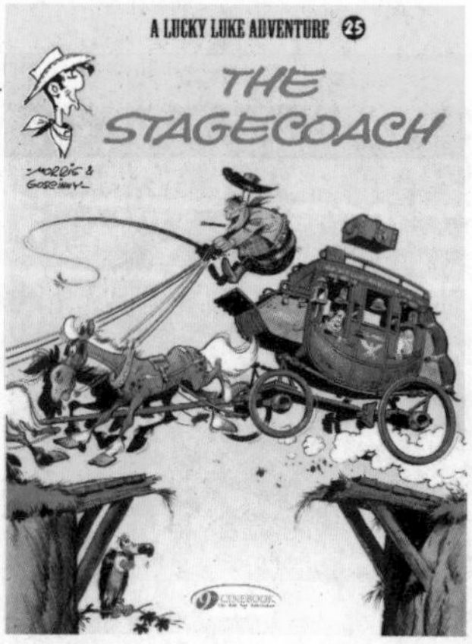
A LUCKY LUKE ADVENTURE 25
THE STAGECOACH
MORRIS & GOSCINNY

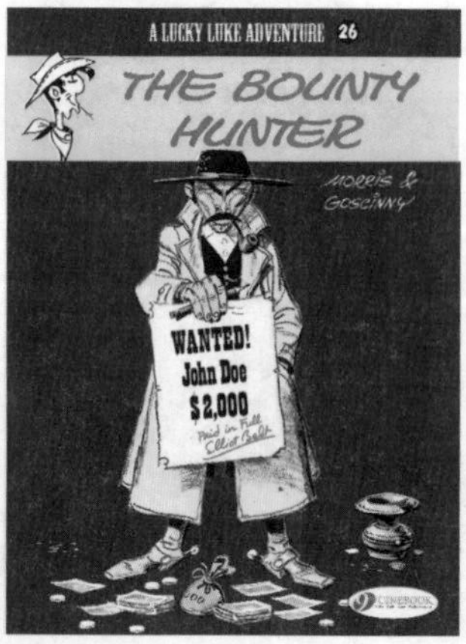
A LUCKY LUKE ADVENTURE 26
THE BOUNTY HUNTER
MORRIS & GOSCINNY
WANTED!
John Doe
$2,000

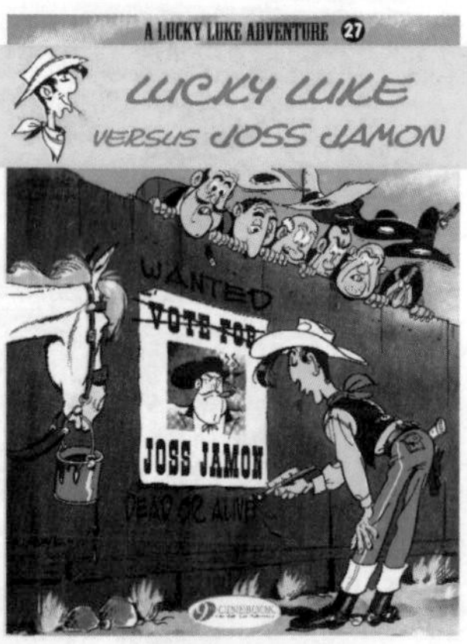
A LUCKY LUKE ADVENTURE 27
LUCKY LUKE VERSUS JOSS JAMON
WANTED
VOTE FOR
JOSS JAMON
DEAD OR ALIVE

FEBRUARY 2011

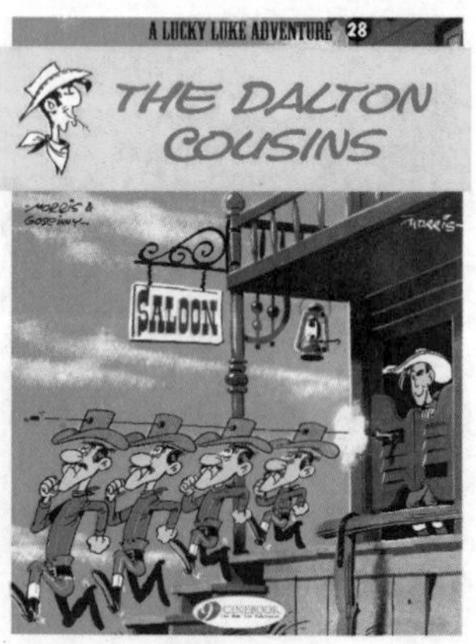
A LUCKY LUKE ADVENTURE 28
THE DALTON COUSINS
MORRIS & GOSCINNY
SALOON

APRIL 2011